'Good evening, Miss Grant.'

Holly had not noticed how deep David's voice was until then. He smiled and her face, already flushed from dancing, deepened in colour as the attractiveness of his smile caught at her heart. She saw the David he might have been at his brother Mike's age, free from the heavy responsibility of the surgeon.

Holly didn't realise how her vitality, her brightness, dimmed her surroundings, but the big man did. The music's tempo changed.

'May I?' He held out his hand. Holly had no option but to accept—he was her ward consultant—so she placed her hand in his and was drawn on to the floor, into his arms. She had never been so close to him, close enough to feel the warmth of his body, notice the extra line or two about his mouth. His nearness excited her and she glanced up into his eyes, hoping he wouldn't sense how he was affecting her.

Patricia Robertson has nursed in hospitals, in District Health, and abroad. Now retired, she is incorporating this past experience in her Medical Romances. She is widowed with two daughters—her hobbies are gardening, reading and taking care of her Yorkshire Terriers. She lives in Scotland, and this is her first story for the Medical Romance list.

DOCTOR TO THE RESCUE

BY

PATRICIA ROBERTSON

MILLS & BOON LIMITED
ETON HOUSE   18–24 PARADISE ROAD
RICHMOND   SURREY   TW9 1SR

All the characters in this book have no existence outside the imagination of the Author, and have no relation whatsoever to anyone bearing the same name or names. They are not even distantly inspired by any individual known or unknown to the Author, and all the incidents are pure invention.

All Rights Reserved. The text of this publication or any part thereof may not be reproduced or transmitted in any form or by any means, electronic or mechanical, including photocopying, recording, storage in an information retrieval system, or otherwise, without the written permission of the publisher.

This book is sold subject to the condition that it shall not, by way of trade or otherwise, be lent, resold, hired out or otherwise circulated without the prior consent of the publisher in any form of binding or cover other than that in which it is published and without a similar condition including this condition being imposed on the subsequent purchaser.

First published in Great Britain 1991 by Mills & Boon Limited

© Patricia Robertson 1991

Australian copyright 1991
Philippine copyright 1991
This edition 1991

ISBN 0 263 77416 3

Set in 10 on 11 pt Linotron Times
03-9110-55162
Typeset in Great Britain by Centracet, Cambridge
Made and printed in Great Britain

CHAPTER ONE

'I want to give up medicine.'

Holly gazed at Michael Quinn, her eyes wide with disbelief.

'Are you sure you know what you're saying? Failing two of your exams isn't a reason to quit. You'll get them on resit.'

An irritated frown furrowed the young man's forehead.

'You sound like David.'

The spring sunshine shone on his pale features, which were set in defiant lines; the mobile mouth compressed, the teeth clenched, even the dark brown hair, ruffled as he ran his fingers through it, seemed rebellious. His resemblance to his older brother was marked, but, where David's face was one of established character, firm mouth, even compelling eyes, Michael's had the softness of youth still about the cheeks and chin.

Holly didn't know David. Staff nurses didn't move in consultants' circles. She just knew of him, that he was an excellent surgeon, quick and competent.

'So you told him?'

Holly was surprised; she knew how in awe of his brother Michael was. She and her friend Angie had tried to help him overcome this fear, but had not succeeded.

She was in Mike's flat, which he shared with another student, John Mitchell. It was superior to most rented accomodation; the armchairs were a little worn but the springs were intact; the brown Dralon had a sad look about it, but there were no holes in the fabric. The patterned carpet was a different colour in places where beer had stained the design, and the curtains could have been brighter, being a dull green.

Mike rose from his chair and paced the room. 'No.' He gave a heavy sigh. 'He'd only treat me like one of his medical students; fix me with an icy stare and say, "Think again,"' Mike impersonated his brother's voice.

Holly looked up at him from her seat on the couch. He was almost as tall as David but not as big; his brother was heavier, more muscular. Holly knew there was a thirteen-year difference between the two men.

Michael sat down beside her, his bony frame hardly moving the seat; Holly was a well-built girl who needed to watch her diet. He searched her face and Holly's heart sank; she knew what he was going to say.

'Holly,' he began tentatively, picking up one of the red curls lying on her shoulder and twining it about his finger but not looking at her, 'I was wondering if you would come with me to tell David.' The words came out in a rush. 'You're so good at that sort of thing.' He let go of the curl and glanced at her face and saw her raise her eyebrows. 'Well. . .' He sighed again. 'You're always joining protest groups,' and as her jaw dropped he added quickly before she could speak, 'Look how you stood up for the junior doctors when they were campaigning for shorter hours.'

'That was different,' she said sharply. 'You can't compare it to what you're asking. Anyway, why don't you ask Angie? She's your girlfriend.'

He grimaced. 'I wanted to see David tonight and I know he won't be in until nine, and Angie starts night duty then.' His face seemed to collapse; the mouth turned down, the brown eyes—his brother's are blue, she thought; now why should I have noticed that?— were doleful.

Compassion for him made her smile. Taking advantage of this softening in her, he said, his face changing from winter to summer, 'I mean, you know what it's like. I remember your telling me how your father wanted you to become a lawyer like himself, but that you wanted to be a nurse and that you——'

Memory of the arguments she'd had with her father and the bitterness of that time made her interrupt him.

'I know, I defied him.' Her eyes became sad as she recalled how her gentle mother had tried to smooth the differences between father and only child. 'It was only Mum's death two years ago that brought us together, and even now we're a bit wary of each other.' She looked affectionately at Mike. 'You don't want friction like that between your brother and yourself, do you?'

'Friction.' He barked out the word and, jumping to his feet, prowled about the room. 'There's been nothing *but* friction between us since our parents died in that freak storm eleven years ago.' He stopped in front of her.

Holly rose and took his hand, but he wrenched it away and crossed to the window. She joined him and stood by his side, looking out at the school yard below, silent now, squashed cartons side by side with empty Coke tins, bits of paper clinging to the railings. It was Monday evening. Mike had begged her to meet him at the flat after she finished in Medical Out-patients at five. 'I must talk to you,' he'd said. 'You'll understand.' She'd wondered what he'd meant. Now she knew.

Holly could see the weather vane topping Harrington General Hospital a block away. The sunshine shone on the cock, which had been adorned at various times with hats, scarves and other articles of clothing by a succession of medical students.

Mike turned towards the redheaded girl with green eyes, which at times he found uncomfortable to meet, they were so clear and honest. A calmness had settled upon him. He shrugged.

'Anyway, David's guardianship finishes on my twenty-first birthday.' His eyes narrowed. 'So he can't threaten to cut off my allowance if I change my course.' It was childishly said. He smiled.

How was it that Holly remembered his brother smiling at a patient he was ushering into his room in Surgical Out-patients?

'Don't you think you should try again?' She felt she must do all she could to dissuade him. 'I've seen you with the patients and you're very good with them. And you are three years into the course.'

His expression became stubborn. 'Oh, there are aspects of medicine that appeal to me, but. . .' He turned from her to gaze into the room and didn't continue.

'What d'you want to do instead?' she asked.

He moved from her side and resumed his restless striding.

'Anything and everything.' He looked back at her, his face alive. 'Travel. Pick up work here and there.' He glanced at the sky behind her. 'Live the life of an adventurer.'

Holly was horrified. What had come over him? She knew he wasn't very mature, but what he was proposing was madness.

'Your brother will have a fit.'

It was the wrong thing to say.

'Good,' he said, but she detected a nervousness behind the defiant word.

He sat on the couch and she crossed to sit beside him. Placing an arm round his shoulders, she said forcefully, 'I do think you should reconsider. You can travel when you've qualified.'

His head jerked up. 'No.' He almost shouted the word. 'I've made up my mind.'

'Are you sure you're not thinking like this just to get back at your brother?' she asked intuitively.

He jumped to his feet. 'Of course not.' He frowned in anger.

His protest was too adamant and convinced Holly that that was the reason for his decision. Her green eyes darkened; her face became stern. 'I think you should give it more thought,' she said, and added, 'I'm not prepared to go with you to see your brother until you do.'

'Oh, all right.' He reached for her hand and pulled her to her feet. 'I'll make you a cup of tea.'

This sudden acceptance of her ultimatum filled her with alarm. She suspected he had no intention of doing as she suggested.

'I won't stop for tea,' she said. 'I must go home.'

As she walked to the bus-stop, Holly thought about him. Zipping up her anorak, she worried about what she should do. The bus drew up with a swish, distracting her thoughts.

They left the town with its red-brick houses and, almost dramatically, were in the country. Moors lay either side of the twisting road. Small flowers presented their bright faces to the oncoming traffic. The greyness of winter was lifting, and she smiled happily as she thought how the land she was looking at would become alive again now that summer was approaching. Mike's face suddenly interposed itself between her and the scenery. What could she do to help him?

The bus stopped, jerking her from her reverie. As she alighted, the clean air, fresh from the moors, brought with it the scent of spring flowers. The village of Sheeplaw was three miles from the town of Harrington but, set as it was on the moors, could have been thirty, it was so peaceful. Her home was just a bit further along the main street.

As she opened the front door the familiar smells of polish, cigars, and the indefinable essence of the old house met her.

She breathed a sigh of contentment. This was her home and she didn't want to live anywhere else. She'd lived in a flat in Harrington while doing her training, more to avoid her father than out of necessity. When she'd qualified she'd found her career had matured her and had asked if her father would mind if she came home. She remembered the day with clarity. She'd gone to his office in the High Street, had even made an appointment. He had stood, tall and broad—he had a figure like David Quinn's. . . There she was again, visualising the consultant. Her father had agreed and smiled. It was the smile she recalled now; it had held a vulnerability which had touched her.

His large shadow stood in the lounge doorway now.

'Hello, Dad,' she said. Normally she didn't kiss him, but today, thinking of Mike's relationship with his brother, she was glad all that friction was behind her and kissed his cheek.

'Thanks,' he said, and the simplicity with which he said it smote her. Was she too hard on him?

'I'll try to make it habit,' she quipped, smiling.

'Mrs Braithwaite left the dinner prepared. It just needs putting in the microwave.'

There was a companionable silence between them as they went into the kitchen. It had been modernised; oak units fitted in successfully with the old house's character. Holly switched on the light and popped the casserole into the microwave.

Her father pulled out a chair and sat down. 'Had a good day?' he asked, accepting a full plate from her.

Should she ask his advice about Mike? But, if she

did, wouldn't it recall their own past differences, which were so like David's and his brother's? It might jeopardise their present easier relationship. She wasn't prepared to risk that so said, 'It was quite busy. How about you?'

They chatted about their work, watched television together and went to bed early.

Sleep eluded her. How could she stop Mike from ruining his life? She turned the pillow to a cooler side, but it didn't help. Perhaps if I go and see David Quinn and prepare him, mention Mike's decision, the consultant would be able to counsel his brother wisely. Yes, that's what I'll do. I'll catch him in Surgical Out-patients, or, better still, when he's leaving. Medical Out-patients overlooked the surgical department, so she'd be able to watch for him.

Next day she spent the latter part of the morning glancing towards the window.

'I know the weather's improving, Staff,' Sister Michaels said, close to her elbow, a sheaf of case-notes in her arms. 'It's supposed to be settled for the day, so perhaps you would take these,' she proffered the pile to Holly, 'to the secretary.' The touch of sarcasm in the sister's voice made Holly reach quickly for the notes.

'Yes, Sister,' she said.

An irritated frown crossed her brow as she headed for the secretary's office. She'd probably miss the consultant now. But as she was returning she saw the distinctive figure of David Quinn coming out of X-ray. Hastening her step, she caught up with him.

'Excuse me, sir,' she said, adjusting her stride to his long one.

He was wearing a grey pinstriped suit and white shirt with his university tie. He looked like a prosperous businessman. The gaze he directed at Holly was that of an alert confidence attained from making many important decisions. His white coat was slung over his shoulder, the colour reflecting on his face, sharpening his features, picking out the lines beside his eyes, the furrows between them. Laughter tempered by sternness, she thought, and hoped it was true.

Holly was five feet seven, but she had to look up at David, who, she realised, was taller than his brother. Must be over six feet, she thought.

'Yes, Staff,' he said, his voice deep and warm as he smiled down at the pretty redhead; he had a preference for blondes.

She had never been this close to him before. Close enough to smell his aftershave, to see the black hair was short, but not short enough to prevent its curling on his collar. An easy smile lighted his eyes, which were of a Mediterranean blue. She was intensely aware of him and very much attracted, so much so that her prepared words deserted her and she blurted out. 'It's about Mike. He wants to give up medicine.'

The pleasant expression left his face. The square jaw tightened, the blue eyes darkened, as if a cloud had come over the sun. He frowned.

'I take it you are referring to my brother Michael?'

Did he always call his brother by his given name? The inconsequential thought flashed through her mind.

His tone was like ice. Holly could see what Mike meant about the medical students, and pitied them.

They were standing in the corridor. A porter, wheeling a patient on a trolley past them, gave a curious glance in their direction.

She straightened her spine and said, 'Yes,' not realising how defiant she looked.

His face paled, though it wasn't with shock but anger. 'If Michael has a problem he knows he can bring it to me.' His words were clipped, his expression disdainful. 'He does not require an emissary, so I don't know what you want.'

'I want to——'

He didn't give her time to explain. 'I don't care what you want,' he said viciously.

He strode away, his white coat flapping on his back, leaving Holly's heart beating in time with the angry tattoo of his steps.

A frown drew her brows together. What a rude man, she thought. He might have heard me out.

As she walked towards Medical Out-patients, she couldn't help thinking that she had made matters worse. David Quinn would be doubly hard on his brother now;

Her footsteps quickened. She had better find Mike and warn him. She would phone his flat from Out-patients.

But when she arrived there Sister Michaels met her, already dressed for going off duty.

'My husband's meeting me early,' she explained. 'See the consultants' rooms are tidy, will you?' She hitched her coat more firmly on to her shoulders. 'Then lock up.' Her round face broke into a smile as she handed over the keys.

'Yes, Sister,' said Holly, accepting them but wailing to herself, This'll mean I'll be late.

Now that the medical staff and the patients had left, the department was quiet. There was an air of waiting about the place, and Holly wondered if the anxiety of the many who passed through its rooms lingered in the corners.

In Sister's office, she reached for the phone and dialled Mike's number. There was no reply.

Holly hurried round the rooms, thinking, He'll probably be in the pub.

She changed out of her uniform and left the Outpatients, carefully locking the door behind her. After hanging the key in the administrator's office she pushed her way through the front door, her feet clipping down the steps.

The pub was across the road from the hospital and was called the Surgeon's Arms. Many a joke had been made of its name. 'I saw you in the Surgeon's Arms,' students had quipped to nurses over the years.

Holly pushed through the doors, coughing as tobacco smoke met her. Searching among the many faces, she was relieved to see Mike's; he was sitting at a table with Angie, his expression carefree. Holly felt awful.

'Gin?' he offered as she sat down beside them.

'Thanks,' she said, and thought, I'll need it.

Angie was drinking orange juice, as she was on duty at nine.

'You're looking tired,' Holly said, noting the dark smudges below her friend's eyes.

'You sure know how to buck a girl up,' said Angie wryly. She was shorter than Holly by an inch or two, with a heart-shaped face and dark hair.

Holly smiled. 'Some men like their women pale and interesting—Mike was only saying so the the other day,' she added slyly.

A blush coloured her friend's cheeks. 'Was he?' Angie was playing with her glass and not looking at Holly, who smiled at the bent head.

Mike appeared with her drink, preventing further conversation between the girls.

Holly took it from him and had a big sip.

'You look as though you needed that,' he said, smiling.

Guilt pricked at her, but before she could confess he said, 'By the way, Holly. . .' his expression was apologetic '. . . I took your advice and decided it would be foolish to give up the three years I've already done. I'm going to stay in medicine.' He glanced at the dark girl sitting beside Holly. 'Angie agrees with you that it was just failing my exams and David's displeasure at my results.' He grimaced ruefully. 'He can be pretty grim at times—that made me think of changing my course.'

'Oh,' she groaned.

Her friends looked at her in concern. 'What's wrong?'

'Everything.' She groaned again, and told them of her encounter with David.

Consternation figured their faces. 'He'll be looking for me,' said Mike, his eyes anxious.

Holly thought for a moment. 'We could. . .'

A shadow fell across the table. All three looked up. David was towering over them. 'I've been looking for you, Michael,' he said, his face stiff. Then he saw Holly. 'You,' he said, his brows thunderous. He looked at his brother as he pointed a finger at Holly. 'This girl told me that you want to give up medicine.' His pinstriped suit looked out of place among the casually dressed crowd in the bar. David's voice was like iron, and as cold.

Mike's colour faded. 'I—I don't want to give up medicine,' said Mike.

Holly knew it was just nervousness that had made Mike speak out like that, just as she had blurted to the consultant earlier, though her flustering had been due to the attraction she had felt for David. She was aware of it now; his nearness excited her in spite of his anger. She caught the shine of his cuff-link as he dropped his arm to his side. His face softened at hearing Mike's denial, and Holly could feel David's relief.

'I knew it couldn't be true,' he said. Then his face stiffened as he looked at her with hard, cold eyes.

He was very formidable and seemed to grow before

her, but it was just his shadow looming above her that created the illusion.

'What was all that about, Miss. . .?' He raised an eyebrow.

'Grant. Holly Grant,' she said, doing some quick thinking. If she told him the truth his anger would be directed at his brother, so she said the first thing that came into her head. 'I did it as a dare.'

The disbelief that figured the consultant's face was reflected on Mike's and Angie's though for different reasons.

'I find it difficult to believe a staff nurse could behave so irresponsibly,' he said. He shifted his gaze to his brother. 'What part have you played in all this?'

'I——'

Angie spoke up. 'He hasn't any part in it. I dared Holly.'

David examined the faces before him, Holly's defiant, Angie's embarrassed, and Mike's. . .? He hadn't seen his brother for some time, and noted now, with concern, how tired and anxious the young man looked. There was something in the soft brown eyes so like their mother's. Surely it wasn't fear?

'Michael,' he said, suspicion rising in his mind.

The struggle Mike was making to overcome his fear was obvious to Holly. She willed him to succeed but suspected it was Angie's holding him tightly by the hand that gave him the courage to lift his chin, look straight into his brother's eyes, and say, 'The girls had nothing to do with it.' His anxiety slipped from him, the worried lines on his face became smooth, and he even looked younger. He was no longer afraid of David. 'They were just protecting me.'

There was a fourth chair at their table. David drew it out and sat down. Conversation flowed about them—'Did you hear. . .?' 'Mavis has given up her job.'

'Another beer?'—but the group at the table heard none of it. Michael was the centre of their concentration.

'Protecting you from what?'

The big man was sitting a little apart from the other three, almost as if in judgement, his face stiff, his eyes cold, his teeth clenched. But Holly thought she detected a touch of vulnerability in the way he held his arms crossed close to his chest.

In the past, whenever David's name was mentioned, Mike would clench his fists, tighten his mouth and frown, but now he was relaxed. It was almost is if the brothers' positions were reversed, and Holly cheered silently to herself.

'From your anger.' Mike's voice was clear, without a tremor.

Even David's replying, 'And why should I be angry?' mounting exasperation clearly marked on his face, didn't affect the new Mike.

'Because I did think of giving up medicine.' The words came out in a rush as if they were glad to be let loose. 'Because I told Holly and wanted her to come with me to tell you.' He took a deep breath and added in a firm voice, 'Because I was afraid of you, and needed moral support.'

The four figures sat as if transfixed, unblinking, unmoving. There was a new strength about the way Mike held his head. He didn't lower his eyes from his brother's. The likeness between them was more marked.

After a moment, David said, 'I see.' His shoulders sagged a little, but that was the only outward sign he gave that his brother's words had shocked him. Taking hold of the table, he pushed himself to his feet. 'You're lucky to have such friends,' he said.

Holly wondered if the other two had detected the

wistfulness in the way David had spoken. Perhaps they had, for they were silent as they watched the tall figure, head and shoulders above most of those in the pub, make his way to the door.

Holly raised her glass to Mike and said, 'Thanks.'

He reached forward and took her hand. 'It's I who should be thanking you.' His other hand still held Angie's. Lifting them both up he said, '"All for one and one for all." Isn't that what the musketeers said?'

Their laughter broke their tension.

Next day Sister Michaels called Holly to her office.

'The SNO has asked me to tell you that she wants you to take over the staff nurse's duties on Male Surgical, ward ten.' She smiled at the redhead. 'I know you'll be pleased because you want to specialise in surgery, don't you, Holly?'

'Yes, Sister.' Holly's return smile was a little strained. David Quinn was the consultant for Male Surgical, ward ten.

CHAPTER TWO

'I DON'T envy you taking over from Ruth Stone.' Angie was sitting up in bed, reaching for the cup of tea Holly was handing to her. She was still tired, even though she had slept well that day.

'Why?' A trigger of alarm sharpened Holly's voice.

Angie took a sip of tea. 'She's the worst staff nurse I've ever come across, and I should know, being the night staff on that ward.' She glanced sympathetically at her friend. 'Rumour has it Sister Nicol asked to have her removed, so you'd better watch your step.' Then she gasped. 'David's the consultant on that ward!'

'So?' Holly crossed her legs, the rough material of her jeans scraping as she did so. 'It shouldn't pose a problem,' she said, airily. 'I won't have much to do with him. Sister Nicol will do the ward rounds.' She became enthusiastic. 'I hear she's an excellent surgical sister and, as my ambition is to be one also, I should gain invaluable experience.'

'But David might blame you for embarrassing him.' Angie played nervously with the teaspoon from her saucer.

'Embarrass him?' Holly rose from the bed, her green eyes angry, her red curls bouncing. 'He should thank me,' she said, looking down at her friend. 'How could he have been so blind all these years?'

'Well, I suppose it must have been worrying, taking the responsibility for an eleven-year-old when he was only twenty-four and just qualified,' said Angie.

Holly smiled at her friend with affection. 'Trust a gentle person like you to think of his side.' She wondered if a few of those lines on David's face were due to Mike.

'Anyway, good luck,' said Angie.

The following day, Holly felt she needed it. Sister Nicol's perfectly sculptured features looked at her coolly when she reported for duty. There was a self-containment about the older woman which was reflected in the neatness of her blue dress and the upswept hair arranged in a French pleat, every strand in place. Even the frilly cap sat at the correct angle. Her skin was pale, almost transluscent. She looked like a piece of Dresden china, a few inches smaller than her staff nurse, with tiny hands and feet. Holly felt like a robust farm-girl beside her, with her well-covered frame, pink cheeks and glowing red hair.

'I've had a good report from Sister Michaels about you, Staff Nurse Grant.' Her tone implied that she would not let this influence her own assessment and this was confirmed when she added, 'I hope I'll be able to endorse it.'

'I'll do my best, Sister,' Holly said, hoping she sounded efficient.

Later in the morning Holly was in the ward when she saw David enter, accompanied by Sister. Holly hurried in the opposite direction, hoping to put off facing him for as long as possible. It was just her luck to slip and fall. Strong surgeon's fingers were the first to grasp her arm and haul her to her feet.

'There's no need for you to run away from me, Miss Grant,' he said drily. 'I don't frighten young women, only young men.' She detected a trace of bitterness in his tone. Perhaps Angie had been right.

She straightened her dress, pushed a loosened grip back into her cap and said, 'I wasn't running away from you.' The lie made her tone sharp, for deceit was not usual for her. It was this man; he seemed to bring out the worst in her.

David was looking particularly handsome. The bitterness had left his face to be replaced with a smile that had warmed many a nurse's heart. However, it was not directed at her but at the ward sister, who had joined them. Christine Nicol had not heard David's words but had heard Holly's. She was not smiling; her expression was stern, even hostile.

'Nurse Grant. I will not tolerate cheek on my ward, particularly to Mr Quinn. Apologise at once.'

Holly faced the surgeon. The amused expression in his eyes added to her aggravation.

'I apologise, sir,' she said in a voice that lacked humility.

The twinkle in David's eyes deepened. 'I accept, and hope you weren't hurt, Staff Nurse.' It was said with exaggerated politeness.

I bet he wishes I'd broken my neck, she thought, but said sweetly, 'No,' adding after a slight pause, 'thank you,' and saw his eyebrow rise at the touch of insolence in the way that she spoke.

'In that case, Nurse——' had Sister deliberately demoted her? Holly wondered '—perhaps you will bring Mr Granger to the treatment-room. I want the house surgeon to see his wound.'

'Yes, Sister.'

Holly was turning away when David said, 'I'll have a look at it, if you like, as I'm here.'

Christine smiled at him. 'Thanks. He has a low-grade pyrexia and I suspect a wound infection.' She glanced at Holly. 'Let Mr Quinn know when you're ready, Nurse, please. Mr Granger's in the convalescent-room.'

'Yes, Sister.'

Holly was glad to leave them and resume her journey down the ward.

'Have a good trip, Staff?' one of the patients called.

She looked towards the young man, who was due to have his stitches removed that morning.

'I think I'll try to avoid any more like that in the future,' she said, smiling, and heard an appreciative laugh from some of the patients.

It was a thirty-two bed ward with a convalescent-room at the end, where those well enough took their meals and watched television. It was divided from the main ward by a half-glass, half-wooden partition that enabled the nurses to observe the patients who were in there.

Holly opened the door. 'Sorry to disturb you, Mr Granger, but it's time for your dressing.'

A redheaded man in his early thirties looked up admiringly. 'A redhead at last,' he said. 'I was beginning to think I was the only one in Yorkshire.'

An easy grin spread across Holly's face. 'There are a few more of us—my father, for one.' She received a smile in reply.

The treatment-room was outside the ward, opposite sister's office. Holly ushered her patient in, explaining, as she did so, what she was going to do.

'Don't worry, Staff, I've had it all before.'

'Mr Quinn wants to see your wound this morning,' she told him as she helped him out of his dressing-gown and hung it on the back of the door.

'Ooooh!' Mr Granger's eyes brightened. 'The *big man* himself!'

'Now, Mr Granger,' she admonished. David's nickname was well-known, but she couldn't allow a patient to be disrespectful.

'Sorry, Staff.' Mr Granger's apology didn't sound

repentant, and Holly had to turn away to hide a smile. She drew the dressing-trolley forward.

'Hop up on the couch.' She helped him, and adjusted the pillows behind his head. Picking up the cellular blanket from the bottom, she laid it across his legs.

Mr Granger had had his spleen removed, following a football accident. She opened his jacket and loosened his dressing.

'I'll just fetch Mr Quinn,' she said.

Holly knocked on the office door and went in.

'Would you please wait for permission to enter?' Christine's voice was cold.

Holly suspected she'd interrupted something, something not to do with the patients.

'Sorry, Sister, but you did ask me to let Mr Quinn know when Mr Granger was ready.'

Her choice of words could have been better—they sounded arrogant. Sister Nicol stiffened. Whoops, thought Holly, I've put up another back.

Before Christine could speak, David drawled, 'I take it that's now,' and pulled his tall frame from his seat.

'Yes, sir.'

Holly was only too pleased to follow him out of the office. In the treatment-room, she washed and dried her hands, opened the dressing pack and tipped it out on to the trolley, conscious all the time of David watching her.

Washing her hands again, she opened the packet, smoothed it out and, taking the forceps, lifted the loosened dressing and dropped it into the bag, explaining to the patient what she was about to do all the time.

It was awful. She felt as if she were taking her practical exam again and was sure he was making her feel like that deliberately. When she dropped a disposable forceps on the floor she heard him tut and, glancing at his face, detected an amused expression there. Was he trying to get his own back? Embarrass her? Well, he wouldn't succeed, but she could feel herself blushing as she looked down at the suture line.

'Well, Staff Nurse Grant? What treatment would you prescribe?'

She glanced up at him. His eyes were amused; he was teasing her. Well, she would show him. Looking down at the inflamed suture line, she said, 'Antibiotics, four-hourly temperature, plenty of fluids and a careful eye kept on the wound.'

He raised his eyebrows; she could almost see him mentally clapping. 'Quite right.' He looked down at the patient. 'I think we'll keep this staff nurse, don't you, Mr Granger?' Holly examined the consultant's face, suspecting he was being sarcastic, but it was bland. It was a genuine compliment. She was inordinately pleased, and showed it by grinning.

'Absolutely, Mr Quinn,' Mr Granger said, and, as David smiled and left them, added, 'We redheads must stick together,' grinning up at her.

She laughed. The tension drained away and she finished the dressing. As she left the treatment-room with the patient, Holly glimpsed the registrar Richard Morris standing with David in the office. She was so intent on watching the doctors that she didn't see the house surgeon, Johnny Simpson, until he said, at her elbow,

'Hi, Holly.'

'You're going to be late,' she whispered, gesturing towards the group.

'Oh, they'll be chatting for ages yet,' he said, unperturbed. He smiled at Mr Granger. 'How's the wound?'

'Staff put me on antibiotics.'

Johnny's eyes widened. 'Trying to get my job?' he teased Holly.

He really was very nice, though too easygoing for her and, in any case, was engaged. She knew him quite well, having worked with him on another ward.

'Mr Quinn saw the wound and prescribed for the patient,' she corrected Mr Granger's statement.

'Did he indeed?' Johnny's surprise was evident. He looked at the patient. 'You were honoured.'

'If you've quite finished chatting,' David's dry voice interrupted them, 'perhaps you'll join us on the round.'

Johnny almost jumped to attention, his tall, bony frame straightening quickly. 'Yes, sir.'

Christine was waiting with the case-note trolley.

'We won't need you, Staff. Perhaps you'd admit the new patients.'

Holly was glad she didn't have to go on the round. The rest of the day passed quickly. She was off at six and didn't realise how tired she was until she stepped out of the hospital. There was always a certain amount of strain attached to starting a new ward; the patients were suspicious of you until they decided what you were like. This time the coolness of the ward sister had added to Holly's tension, and the presence of David Quinn had increased her stress. She couldn't wait to feel the air from the moors on her face.

Later that evening Angie phoned. 'How did you get on?' she asked.

'OK, I suppose. Sister was a bit stiff.'

'Well, I did warn you. I expect she'll change when she finds out what a good nurse you are,' Angie encouraged. 'What I really rang for was to ask if you would like to change in my room on the night of Mike's twenty-first party. I meant to ask you the other evening, but. . .' There was no need for her to explain. 'By the way, how did you get on with David?'

Holly didn't know quite how to answer, so said, 'I hardly saw him. Will he be at Mike's disco party?'

'As he's paying for it, I expect he'll make a token visit, but I don't think it's quite his cup of tea.'

A vision of David in knife-edged trousers and spotless shirt disco-dancing with their friends made Holly laugh.

'Share the joke,' Angie pleaded.

Something stopped Holly painting the ridiculous picture for her friend, and she said, 'There isn't one really.' Then, to ensure Angie didn't persist, she added, 'I'd like to take you up on your offer. I could bring my clothes in the day before, if that's all right?'

'That'll be fine.'

Holly was on at one o'clock the following day. She was carrying the case-notes for the anaesthetist, who was to examine the patients scheduled on tomorrow's list. They were about to enter the ward when a middle-aged man approached them. Holly smiled encouragingly at the flustered face.

'I'm sorry I couldn't get here yesterday. Am I too late?'

He was of medium height with greying hair; his bushy eyebrows twitched as he talked and worry lines furrowed his forehead.

'You must be Mr Moore,' Holly said gently.

'Staff! Don't delay Dr Patterson, he's a busy man. I'll attend to this patient.' Sister Nicol came out of the office, her figure rigid, her expression disapproving.

'Very good, Sister.'

'And when you've finished assisting him please check the preps have been done properly.'

Holly nodded.

'What have you done?' Tom Patterson smiled at the redhead.

'Nothing yet,' she grinned.

She was drawing the curtains back from around Mr

Russell's bed—he was scheduled for a bronchoscopy—when Nurse Bailey, the junior nurse, came up to her.

'S-Sister says Mr Moore's ready for Doctor Patterson,' she stammered.

Holly's smile was gentle as she said to the young nurse, 'Thanks.'

The anxious expression faded from Jean Bailey's face.

'I don't expect you were as nervous as that when you were a first-year nurse, Staff?' Tom was watching the retreating figure.

'Nurse Bailey will make a fine nurse one day. She only lacks confidence.' Holly wasn't going to tell him she had been just like the junior when she started on her first ward.

He grinned. 'Mother hen looking after her chicks?'

The anaesthetist was the same height as Holly. She looked into the amused brown eyes level with her own.

'That's Sister Nicol's job,' she replied. 'But it'll be mine one day.'

His expression changed to one of discernment. 'I can well believe it.'

They went across to Mr Moore. Holly drew the curtains around his bed and introduced the anaesthetist.

'I'm just going to listen to your chest,' explained the doctor.

The patient sneezed. 'Oh, sorry, Doctor.'

The anaesthetist frowned. 'Have you got a cold?'

Mr Moore's bushy eyebrows drew together. 'I had a sore throat yesterday and I have been sneezing.'

Tom Patterson put his stethoscope back into his pocket. 'I'm afraid you won't be able to have your hernia repaired until your cold's better,' he told Mr Moore.

'But, Doctor. . .' anxiety flared in the patient's eyes '. . . I've taken time off work especially for it.'

Tom Patterson looked sympathetic, but said, 'We can't give you an anaesthetic if you have a cold.'

'But why?'

'If I anaesthetised you in your present condition you would develop pneumonia,' he explained patiently.

They left a very disconsolate patient and returned to the office. Tom's eyebrows rose and fell when he saw David lounging in the spare chair—he should have been in Out-patients.

'Glad you're here, David,' he said. 'We can't do Mr Moore tomorrow; he's got a cold.'

Christine Nicol frowned. 'He didn't mention it to me.'

'Probably didn't know he couldn't have an anaesthetic if he had a cold,' Tom said. 'Quite a few people don't.'

David stood up. 'I'll have a word with him.'

Holly was surprised. Consultants usually left their housemen to explain.

Christine saw her staff nurse hovering. 'I'm sure you've something to do, Staff.'

David held the door for Holly and, as she passed in front of him, she understood why he was called the big man—he nearly filled the door-frame.

'Thank you,' she said accepting the courtesy.

Holly checked to see if the preps were completed, informing the second-year nurse that Mr Moore was off the operation list. It was nearly three o'clock and the visitors would be here in a moment. Her eyes travelled over the ward, checking to see if it was tidy and, as they did so, caught a glimpse of David smiling down at Mr Moore. She noticed how the strong lines of David's face had softened, making him look younger. I wonder what he's really like? she thought.

Christine was off at five. After she had given the report to Holly, she said, 'I've checked the consent for operation forms have been signed. Please impress upon the night staff that those for surgery are not to have anything to eat or drink and that their water-jugs are to be removed from their lockers.' She drummed her biro to emphasis each word.

Tired smudges below the blue eyes roused Holly's compassion. She knew what a heavy responsibility running an acute surgical ward could be.

Holly smiled and said, 'Yes, Sister.'

Christine's face didn't soften. 'See that you do, then.'

It was a relief when she left. Holly went to check that Mr Moore's bed had been made up with fresh linen. He was to be admitted next week.

'Staff,' one of the new patients called.

Holly crossed over to him. He was standing beside his bed. In his mid-thirties, he was to have a partial gastrectomy the following day.

'Can I help, Mr Johnstone?' she asked, smiling encouragingly.

There was a worried frown on his face as he glanced up and down the ward. 'Staff. . .' He hesitated, an embarrassed blush colouring his face.

'Yes?' She touched his arm.

His Adam's apple moved up and down as he swallowed.

'The anaesthetic. Is it safe?' he whispered.

'Of course, Mr Johnstone,' she reassured him, keeping her voice low. 'Dr Patterson's an experienced anaesthetist. You'll be given a small injection in your arm, here in the ward, before you go to Theatre,' she explained. 'It will relax you.' She smiled gently. 'And Mr Quinn is an excellent surgeon.' Enigmatic, she thought, but his knife-work was exceptional.

Mr Johnstone still looked worried. 'Oh, I have no

doubts about Mr Quinn. He explained the operation in simple terms so that I would understand.' Admiration for the surgeon glowed in the patient's eyes.

It's a shame David doesn't apply the same intuitiveness where his brother is concerned, was the thought that flitted through her mind.

'I suppose you must think it's silly, a grown man being afraid.' He looked embarrassed.

She hurried to reassure him. 'Of course not. It's natural.' Holly glanced round the ward. 'I bet all those going to Theatre for the first time feel the same.'

His face relaxed. 'D'you think so, Staff?'

'I know so.' And the truth behind her words lay in her expression.

He believed her and smiled. 'Thanks. You've been very kind.'

To know she had helped lift his anxiety gave Holly immense pleasure. She couldn't think of any other job that would be so satisfying.

Her heart was happy as she went about the routine work; taking temperatures, writing up the Kardex, giving out the medicines. Everything took a little longer. Being new to the ward meant that she had to find where things were kept.

Holly was just putting the top on her pen when the office door opened. She turned with a smile, expecting to see the night staff, but it was Christine Nicol, her blonde hair loose about her shoulders, a chic black dress clinging to her perfect figure, a short jacket of the same colour draped over her arm. She looked willowy and feminine. Behind her was David Quinn, his white shirt bright against the blackness of his suit. He looked magnificent. Incredibly handsome.

Holly's mouth went dry; her pulse quickened. A stab of jealousy caught her unexpectedly. She quickly suppressed it. What was it to her if David took Christine out?

'I thought I would come and see how you were getting on.'

Christine's words stilled Holly's heart and swept her errant thoughts aside. She was filled with resentment at the implied doubt of her ability, and knew her feelings were reflected on her face when she saw David smile.

Christine had lifted the Kardex. 'You've forgotten Mr Allen's enema.' Her voice was so sharp that it seemed to cut the air.

Holly looked directly at her. 'I think, if you turn the card, you'll find it has been requested,' she said, the tone of her voice impersonal.

Christine blushed, but even that was a delicate shade of pink. Why can't I look like that instead of appearing as large as life and just as bright? Holly thought, envying the blonde woman.

'Oh.' Christine turned the card. 'So it has.' She was completely unruffled.

Holly could feel David's eyes upon her, and glanced in his direction. He was leaning against the wall, his arms crossed, looking bored, but Holly sensed he was curious to see how she would react.

Christine replaced the Kardex on the desk. A knock was followed by the entrance of the night nurses. It broke the tension. Their chattering stopped abruptly when they saw David and Christine. Angie wasn't dismayed, though.

'Good evening, sir,' she greeted David cheerfully, and smiled at Christine.

He smiled back and said, taking Christine's arm, 'I think it's time we said goodnight.'

As the door closed behind the couple Angie let out a 'phew'.

'You can say that again,' agreed Holly.

Later, hurrying from the hospital to catch her bus, she saw its rear lights disappearing down the road.

'Oh,' she groaned, knowing another half-hour would elapse before the next one. It was starting to rain and she hadn't an umbrella.

A silver Rover drew up beside her and David said, 'Can I give you a lift?'

She would have liked to refuse, but her legs were aching and she longed for the comfort of her home, so she said, 'I live at Sheeplaw.'

'I know. Hop in.'

Holly wondered where Christine was, but, as she settled into the passenger-seat, it was almost as if the blonde woman were with them. Her perfume seemed to linger in the car's fabric.

'Did Mike tell you where I live?' She was curious to know. It came out bluntly. His nearness was disconcerting her. His bulk, in silhouette, was so close.

'Your father's my lawyer.' He paused to negotiate a corner, his hands firm on the wheel. 'We're members of the same club, and I see him there sometimes.'

'I didn't know.'

'That's not surprising.' He gave her a quick glance. 'You don't seem to spend much time with him, do you? He strikes me as a very lonely man.'

Part of Holly's reluctance to accept David's lift was because she'd thought he would mention her part in Mike's rebellion. So the unexpectedness of his words shocked her, and then angered her.

'You're an authority, of course.' Her voice was heavy with sarcasm. 'Mike's a shining example of *your* companionship.'

She knew she would regret what she had said later, but the stress of the day, the attraction she felt for him, and her tiredness, made her rash.

They had left the town behind. The dashboard lights

didn't allow her to see his expression. The high beam lit the road and a rabbit was caught, stunned to immobility.

David swerved to avoid it.

'The cases are hardly similar.' His voice came sharply out of the gloom.

'No?' She could not help herself from saying, 'You are his father figure. At least I'm not afraid of mine.'

She knew she had gone too far when he stopped the car with a jerk, flinging her forward. Only the seatbelt prevented her hitting the windscreen.

His dark shadow turned to face her and she could feel the strength of his anger. 'I would throw you out of the car, here and now, if you weren't a woman.' Each word came out hard and clipped. 'But even I, monster that I am,' his tone was biting, 'wouldn't leave a defenceless woman alone on the moors.'

Goaded by his words, she said, 'I can take care of myself,' and fumbled for the door-handle. His arm shot in front of her and she heard a snap as he pressed down the lock.

'If you're not careful I'll treat you like a father and put you over my knee and spank you.'

She knew his threat was real and edged away a little from him. Only the sound of the engine filled the silence as he started it up and they drove on.

Holly used the minimum of words to point out her house. 'That one with the porch light on.'

He stopped. She jumped out, key in hand, and didn't wait to watch him drive away.

CHAPTER THREE

'HI, HOLLY.' Mike caught up with her in the corridor next day as she was going on duty. There was a new confidence about him; the hesitancy in his eyes had gone.

'You're looking pleased with yourself.' She smiled, delighted at his transformation.

His face lit up. 'David came to see me last night at about ten o'clock.' He sounded surprised. 'He's never done that before. Asked if I'd like to play squash with him next week.' He smiled. 'Of course, I said yes.' Then a little doubt crept into his voice as he added, 'I only hope I can give him a good match.'

'You will,' Holly reassured him. 'You're an excellent player.'

Mike grimaced. 'He's stronger, though.'

'You're quicker.' She had to boost his confidence; it would never do for him to slip now.

'Would you come along and watch?' Holly was pleased to hear it was a genuine request and not a plea for help.

'When it is?'

'Monday, four o'clock.'

'Sorry, I'm on duty.' And she was glad she had a genuine excuse. She didn't want to see David in a social setting.

They had reached the ward corridor. 'See you at the party on Saturday,' he said as he left her.

'I wouldn't miss that,' she called after him.

She watched his lean figure, his student coat flapping

about his legs, stride down the corridor. His walk has changed; it's more positive, she thought.

The office seemed full of pale blue dresses. She was the last to arrive. After the report had been taken and the night staff had gone to a well-earned rest, Christine said, 'As the list is starting early today, the first pre-med's been given, so I want. . .' she fixed her nurses with a stern eye '. . .no slip ups.'

Operation day was always busy, but the routine work still had to be done. Holly admired the efficient way Christine organised her staff. I wish she had confidence in me, was the wistful thought that passed through her mind. Then she cast it aside. I'll just have to prove how competent I am.

Towards the end of the morning she was making a post-operative bed when Jean Bailey came over to her.

'Mr Johnstone's becoming restless and is moving his arm with the drip in it.' Suppressed anxiety made her voice quiver.

Holly smiled reassuringly and went with the junior to the patient's bedside. She'd left the young nurse alone with Mr Johnstone, thinking the responsibility would encourage her.

When they reached him he was pale, a thin film of perspiration dampened his upper lip and his face was pinched and worn. Holly knew what was wrong.

'Have you a lot of pain?' she asked gently.

He tried to smile but couldn't answer; a spasm crossed his face and more perspiration appeared on his brow.

'Help me make Mr Johnstone more comfortable, Nurse,' she said.

David Quinn seemed to materialise from nowhere.

'I think the patient would benefit more from his post-op injection.' He was wearing Theatre greens—they made his figure look larger than ever. He was studying the temperature and blood-pressure chart. 'Judging by these readings, he's in quite a bit of pain.' He fixed Holly with a frowning stare.

His assumption that she was unaware of her patient's needs struck at her professional pride. 'I know that, sir, and was just about to attend to it.'

Jean Bailey's mouth shaped a silent 'oooh' behind the consultant's back.

David's face tightened and his black brows drew together, but she did not flinch.

'I'm sure that's not how you were taught to answer a consultant, Nurse Grant.'

He was doing Sister Nicol's trick—demoting her.

He was intimidating, and Holly could feel her legs tremble, but her gaze didn't falter. Why shouldn't she speak out?

His face became grimmer when she did not apologise. His blue eyes were cold, but they softened as he looked at the patient. 'We'll soon fix your pain,' he said, and left them without glancing at Holly.

'Stay with Mr Johnstone,' she told Nurse Bailey, whose pale face had become paler.

I seem to make a habit of embarrassing him, Holly thought as she followed in his footsteps. Thank goodness he was not in the office when she reported Mr Johnstone's rise in pulse, tense face and restlessness. The blonde head looked up.

'Oh, yes,' Christine said. 'I was just getting his notes ready. Mr Quinn told me.' Her expression was composed; she even gave Holly a small smile.

So David hadn't reported her rudeness. Holly was relieved.

'Check it for me, will you, Staff?' Christine was at the drug cupboard.

Holly hurried back to the patient with the prepared

injection, administered it, and stayed with Mr Johnstone until he settled.

That Sunday she was off. Remembering her conversation with David, she spent it with her father. They walked on the moors, had a pub lunch and enjoyed a companionable evening watching television.

She felt more aware of her father than she had been for some time. How young she had been all those years ago, and how cruel. She had not considered if her biting words would hurt him. She had been so righteous. Perhaps if they had discussed her wish to join the nursing profession calmly they would not have become estranged.

On Monday morning, when she reported for duty, she found that Mr Moore had been admitted as an emergency and was in Theatre.

'When he returns I want you to special him, Staff.'

Holly had just finished taking the temperatures when the trolley with the patient arrived. Once he was settled in bed, she wrapped the cuff of the blood-pressure machine round his upper arm. Christine came to the bedside with the TPR and fluid-balance charts.

'He'll need quarter-hourly aspirations for the time being, then half-hourly, depending on what is coming up.' She pressed the plaster holding the Ryle's tube in place more firmly on to his cheek, glancing up at the blood transfusion as she did so. 'I'll look back shortly to see how you're getting on.' Christine was not patronising, she was just detailing the routine procedure following abdominal surgery.

Mr Moore's chest wheezed. 'Mr Quinn's already asked the physiotherapist to come,' she said.

Holly nodded, feeling more relaxed with Christine than she had since she'd started on ward ten.

Nurse Bailey approached Holly as she was standing at the foot of the bed writing up the charts.

'I thought Mr Moore wasn't being admitted until Wednesday,' she said quietly.

Holly glanced sideways at her. 'So he was, but his hernia strangulated.' And when the first-year nurse looked puzzled, explained, 'You know how a hernia is formed when a sac of peritoneum, containing in this case a piece of bowel, pushes through a weak spot in the abdominal muscle?' And when Jean nodded she continued, 'Well, in Mr Moore's case, the gut was nipped by the neck of the sac and the blood supply cut off, causing strangulation.'

Jean's face cleared. 'Thanks, Staff,' she said, then asked, 'Why isn't Mr Moore in Intensive Care?'

'They haven't any room for him.' She smiled. 'They want to increase our work-load.' It was said as a joke.

Her voice had been low, but not low enough, for David Quinn had heard but not seen the smile. Did he always appear from nowhere like a genie? He must have thought she was complaining, for he said, 'Will that be a problem, Miss Grant?' His tone implied that her supposition was correct.

She turned her head to face him. 'No, sir.' She didn't even blush.

Jean slipped away. Holly handed him the charts. He glanced at the recordings and then at the patient. Mr Moore had his eyes closed, but they opened when the consultant's fingers felt for the radial pulse.

'Everything went very well, Mr Moore.' The quiet assurance in David's voice was reflected in his eyes.

You could be warmed by such confidence. You could rest easy with this man, knowing he would protect you. The knowledge flashed through her mind.

Suddenly she wanted his approbation, wanted to be friends, wanted. . .wanted. . .more? Her pulse quickened.

'The physiotherapist is coming to clear your chest. She'll give you breathing exercises.'

David's words jerked Holly from her reverie. She watched the anxious lines about the patient's mouth relax—he even managed to smile.

'Thanks, Doctor.' His voice was husky, his mouth dry.

Holly reached for the oral tray. David patted Mr Moore's hand. 'Make sure he's kept pain-free,' he said, giving Holly a sharp stare.

She snatched the charts he was holding out to her.

'We'll do our best to make Mr Moore comfortable,' she said. Holly wasn't going to let David undermine her confidence.

He shook his head ever so slightly and she thought she heard a 'tut, tut'. It was almost as if he had wagged a finger at her. What an aggravating man he was. How could she have felt drawn to him a moment ago?

Her eyes followed him down the ward. As he reached the doors he looked back at her, and she was sure he was smiling.

Banishing him from her mind, she concentrated on taking Mr Moore's blood-pressure and pulse. Then she aspirated the Ryle's tube and had just finished when the physiotherapist arrived.

'I'm going to give you a few breathing exercises.' Irene Hall smiled down at Mr Moore. She was a tall, slim young woman with brown hair and hazel eyes, which were set in a plain face. She was very competent at her job.

Holly helped to support the patient as Irene assisted him to breathe.

Later that morning the third-year nurse took over specialling Mr Moore so that Holly could go to lunch. She was to relieve Christine afterwards.

Promptly at one o'clock Holly entered the office.

David Quinn was lounging in the spare chair, his legs crossed and his foot, in its polished black shoe, swinging.

Holly knew his eyes were following her as she took the report, and found it difficult to concentrate. His personality was so strong that it seemed to fill the office. His grey-suited arm lay along the side of the desk; his manicured hand, supple as a woman's but strong as a man's, hung over the end. There was a scar on the middle finger.

'Nurse Grant.' Christine's voice was sharp.

'Sorry, Sister.' Holly tried to dismiss the consultant—pretend he wasn't there.

As David left with Christine, Holly wondered afresh about their relationship. Rumours had it they were 'just good friends', but he certainly seemed attentive. The thought nagged at her for the rest of her time on duty.

The day of Mike's twenty-first birthday arrived. During the morning Sister sent Holly to collect the case-notes for a new patient admitted straight from Casualty with a brachial aneurysm; David Quinn had them in Outpatients.

Holly knocked on the surgical consultant's door. Sister Rose, as pink and pleasant as her name, opened it, an enquiring expression on her face.

'Sister Nicol would like Mr Stead's notes, please, Sister. Mr Quinn has them.'

Sister left the door partially open as she went to fulfil Holly's request. David was sitting behind his desk with a middle-aged woman in the chair opposite. Even at that distance, Holly could see the faded gentility which clung to the patient.

'There isn't any reason for you to be late, Mrs

Turner.' David's voice was stern. 'The buses run a regular service and stop outside the hospital.'

'Well. . .' Holly could feel the grey-haired woman's embarrassment. '. . . I didn't have the bus fare.' There was a tremor in her voice. 'It was just a neighbour's kindness that enabled me to get here now.' Mrs Turner was twisting the handles of her shabby bag.

David glanced up at Sister Rose hovering at his elbow. 'Yes, Sister?' There was a frown of annoyance on his face.

'Staff's come for Mr Stead's notes, sir.'

He picked them from a pile on his desk and thrust them at her, then turned to the patient.

'The Department of Health and Social Security will provide you with the fare.'

'Well. . .' Mrs Turner's voice was quiet '. . . I like to be independent.'

'You've paid your National Insurance—you're entitled to it.'

Holly didn't hear the softening in his voice because Sister Rose was saying, 'Here you are, Staff,' and was handing over the notes.

Holly made her way back to the ward in a shocked state. She had been impressed with David's manner towards the patients on the ward. She knew he could be intimidating—the medical students and herself had experienced that—but how could he treat that nice woman so harshly? Was he so unintuitive? Holly had met others like Mrs Turner—too proud to accept what they thought of as charity from the DHSS. David must have also.

She went about the jobs Sister had assigned her; preparing Mr Stead for Theatre and doing the dressings. All the time her disappointment with David Quinn lingered with her. She tried to push it from her mind, but it kept coming back. Why am I thinking about him like this? she wondered as she re-stocked the treatment-room with dressing packs, viciously slapping one on top of the other. He means nothing to me. But a vision of his face with its clean-cut jaw, blue eyes and generous mouth rose between her and the cupboard door she had just closed. So he was a handsome, attractive, sexually appealing male. So what?

Holly lifted the treatment book and went back to the office, hoping he wouldn't be there. This time it was empty.

The Saturday of the party she was on duty until nine. Angie had given her the key to her room, where Holly had left her clothes.

As she slipped the black full-skirted dress over her head she wondered if David would appear at the party. Critically she surveyed herself in the mirror and twirled. As she stopped, the soft folds caressed her legs. The bodice was fitted, the sleeves three-quarter-length. She smiled at her reflection. She liked this dress; she felt comfortable in it.

Searching in her bag, she found her brush and applied it vigorously until her hair bounced and shone about her shoulders.

Satisfied with her appearance, she pulled on a black coat, slipped on suede shoes, picked up her clutch-bag and left the nurses' home.

Hanleys, where the disco was to be held, was within walking distance.

When she arrived she left her coat with the cloak-room attendant and pushed open the door into the disco area. Loud music greeted her.

'Hi, Holly.' 'Make way for the worker.' Friends hailed her and she smiled in reply.

One of the veterinary students grabbed her hand and whisked her on to the dance-floor. 'Haven't seen you for ages, Andrew,' she said. She liked the hazel eyes smiling into hers and the companionable red hair.

'I've been so busy, what with studying and helping Dad on the farm, that I've not had any time to socialise.'

Andrew was a friend of Mike's. She had met him at various student functions. He was stockily built and about her own height of five feet seven, maybe an inch taller, easygoing and likeable.

He swung her away into a twirl, which flared her skirt, showing off her good legs. She saw his grin broaden in appreciation as he eyed her legs. They both laughed. Catching her hand, he drew her back towards him, and it was then that she saw David Quinn standing with Mike at the bar. Immaculate in grey trousers and shirt that couldn't have come from a chain store, David was watching her. Holly saw how the young women nearest to him were trying to attract his attention.

When she record finsihed, Holly dragged Andrew towards the brothers, saying, 'I haven't wished Mike a happy birthday yet.' She gave him a kiss on the cheek as she congratulated him.

'Thanks for the pen, Holly,' he said. 'I'll think of you when I use it.'

'Good evening, Miss Grant.'

Holly had not noticed how deep David's voice was until then. He smiled, and her face, already flushed from dancing, deepened in colour as the attractiveness of his smile caught at her heart. She saw the David he might have been at Mike's age, free from the heavy responsibility of the surgeon.

Holly didn't realise how her vitality, her brightness, dimmed her surroundings, but the big man did.

The music's tempo changed.

'May I?' He held out his hand.

She had no option but to accept—he was her ward

consultant—so she placed her hand in his and was drawn on to the floor and into his arms.

Holly had never been so close to him, close enough to feel the warmth of his body, notice the extra line or two about his mouth. His nearness excited her, and she glanced up into his eyes, hoping he wouldn't sense how he was affecting her. There was an amused twinkle in their blue depth. It was enough.

'Sister Nicol not with you this evening?' she asked sweetly.

'Trying to embarrass me?' The laughter was in his voice this time.

She blushed, but answered boldly and truthfully, 'No, just curious,' and wished she could think before she blurted out like that.

'You certainly deserve full marks for inventiveness.' He laughed.

She was glad he wasn't cross, and grinned back at him cheekily.

The changing disco lights altered the colour of her hair—now red, now green, now blue. Her face had an endearing impishness about it so that his arm tightened about her in more of a hug than a hold. His blue eyes darkened; his head drew closer to hers.

The face raised to his softened as she responded to their sudden rapport. She waited for his kiss, wanted it. He smiled gently in recognition. Then the music changed to the familiar bars of 'The Locomotion', and the spell was broken and split them apart.

To cover her confusion she threw herself into the dance expecting him to leave the floor, but he remained beside her, joining in with gusto. The elation roused by being in his arms still lingered with her and the tempo of the music excited her further. She laughed and threw back her head, sending her curls flying; they swung like golden lights in the wind. She saw desire flare in David's eyes and forgot his involvement with Christine and her disappointment in him professionally.

When the record faded and a new tune blared forth, she was drawn into dancing with others and searched among the weaving bodies to see if David had left the floor. He was still there, claimed by another and smiling down at his partner as he had smiled at her.

Holly pushed a feeling of desolation deep down inside her. It had been foolish to think he had found her special. It had been the music; it had excited them both, and she had imagined his smile or read more into it than had been there.

Andrew appeared beside her. She turned to him and found comfort in the honest face, the smiling eyes. She felt no tension in his arms, nor excitement either. She could relax with him.

As he swung her round Holly caught sight of David. He seemed to be enjoying himself. She heard him laugh quite a few times and wondered if he would ask her to dance again, but he didn't.

The disco finished at one o'clock. Half the guests had already left.

'How are you getting home?' Andrew asked, his arm still round her waist.

She was about to tell him she would ring for a taxi when David spoke from behind her. 'I'm running Miss Grant to Sheeplaw.'

Holly swung towards him. 'I thought you'd gone.' Then she blushed with annoyance. He'd know she had been looking for him.

But he didn't seem to notice. 'I didn't want to leave you stranded. Mike told me you walked from the hospital.' He glanced at Andrew. 'You see, I feel responsible for Miss Grant. She's the staff nurse on my ward.'

Holly's heart-rate had increased when he had made the offer, but it regained its normal rhythm now; he sounded like her father. After all, he was twelve years older than she was, so perhaps he thought of her like that. Then she remembered the way he had looked at her and discarded the thought. David Quinn would never think of a woman like that unless, of course, it was his own daughter.

'Well, in that case...' Andrew said, reluctantly conceding. He turned to Holly and his eyes brightened. 'I'll phone you.'

She had almost forgotten he was there, and was immediately contrite. She put more enthusiasm than she'd intended into her, 'Yes, please do. I'll look forward to it.'

'He seems a nice young man,' David said as he watched the retreating figure. 'A good marriage prospect, I should think.'

Well, she thought, and said, knowing it would annoy him, 'That's the sort of remark I would expect from my father,' and was pleased to see she was right when he replied,

'I'm not that old.'

Holly pretended to study his face. None of the softness of youth lingered there. Lines of laughter and sadness were etched beside the eyes and mouth. The forehead was furrowed, but not as deeply as it would be in later years. And there was a 'presence' about him that she hadn't observed before. Here was a mature man, whose experience of life had left him very sure of himself.

'Have you reached any conclusions?' His eyes were amused but there was a touch of vulnerability about the mouth. Perhaps he wasn't as assured as she had first thought. A sensitive man lay behind the confident façade, so why had he treated Mrs Turner so thoughtlessly?

She pushed the thought away. His unkindness didn't have to be hers. So, smiling up at him, her eyes warm with compassion, she said, 'Yes. My diagnosis is that you'll never be a father figure to any woman.'

He smiled broadly. 'You should have been a doctor.'

'No, thanks.' She laughed. 'Too much responsibility.'

He caught hold of her arm. 'Come on. Let's find your coat.'

CHAPTER FOUR

A WEEK later, Holly was pushing the dressing trolley back to the treatment-room when Irene Hall, the physio, caught up with her.

'How would you like to help us raise money for a scanner? The maternity unit's desperate for one.'

Holly didn't answer immediately; she was trying to negotiate the trolley through the door. Once inside and with it pushed into its place, she turned and said, 'I'd love to. What would you like me to do?'

'Think up events that can be sponsored, and organise them.'

'Is that all?' Holly's voice was wry.

Irene blushed. 'You'll have help.' She sounded defensive. 'A meeting's been planned for seven-thirty tomorrow evening. Will you be able to come?'

After a moment to think Holly answered, 'Yes.'

'Good.' Irene seemed in a hurry to leave.

Left on her own, Holly cleaned the trolley and placed more packs on the bottom shelf.

As she continued with the dressings she wondered who she would be paired with.

'Something on your mind, Staff?' Mr Moore had developed a chest infection which had prevented his discharge. Only Irene's conscientious physiotherapy combined with antibiotics were ensuring his recovery.

Holly smiled. 'Sorry, Mr Moore. I was just thinking about fund-raising,' and she told him about the scanner.

'Mrs Moore would be glad to help,' he said. 'She's a super cook.'

'Great. We'll need all the help we can get.'

Back in the treatment-room at the end of the dressing round, she was just checking the number of packs that were left when Christine came in with David.

'Ask Colonel Sanderson to come here, please, Staff,' she said.

David was pushing an X-ray film in front of the lighted box and didn't look at Holly.

She left them standing close together, arm touching arm. Were they lovers? she wondered.

Colonel Sanderson was in the side-ward. 'Mr Quinn would like to see you in the treatment-room, Colonel,' she said after knocking.

An anxious expression crossed his face and his jaw tightened. 'Are my X-ray results here, Staff?'

'Yes,' she said gently.

Eagerly he asked, 'Have you seen them?'

She was glad she could answer, 'No. Mr Quinn was just putting them up on the X-ray box.'

His face flushed; even his balding head became pink, the remaining grey hairs smartly brushed. He was very particular about his appearance and pressed his trousers every night under the mattress. He looked younger than his sixty-nine years.

I hope the news is good, Holly prayed as she escorted him out of the room. She was about to leave him at the treatment-room door when he said, 'Would you come with me, Staff?' The words were tentatively spoken. She felt even more sorry for him, but didn't show it by her expression.

'Of course I'll come with you,' she said brightly.

He was a head taller than she, but there was a similarity about them, an indomitable spirit common to them both. That was what David Quinn recognised when they entered.

Holly was surprised to see a faint blush touch David's

cheeks and was sure she heard his quick intake of breath, but attributed it to the difficult task ahead of him. The news must be bad, then.

'We won't need you, Staff,' Christine said.

'I'd like Staff Nurse Grant to stay,' Colonel Sanderson said, giving Christine a look which must have quelled many a junior officer.

The colonel was known to be irascible and difficult to please. Holly had admitted him three days ago and an immediate rapport had been felt by both.

Christine's expression froze into a polite smile. Holly drew forward a chair for the colonel, but he ignored it. How she wished she could take his hand, though she knew he would resent it.

His back was stiff, his face rigid as he looked into David's steady eyes.

'The X-ray has confirmed my tentative diagnosis, John,' the surgeon said. 'There is a carcinoma in the bowel.'

Holly was shocked by his bluntness and remembered Mrs Turner.

John Sanderson squared his shoulders. 'In a way, it's a relief.'

'I thought it would be.' David's voice was gentle.

'What happens now, then?'

David closed his eyes for a moment. When they opened they were clear blue and alert. 'Operation. We may get away with removing the affected piece of colon; it's called a hemicolectomy.' He paused, and Holly knew intuitively that a knot of tension lay behind the calm face. What he had to say was not going to easy.

Compassion for the doctor's difficulty swelled her heart. David glanced towards her, almost as if he sensed her sympathy. Perhaps he took strength from that, for his voice became firm.

'If this is not possible we'll have to take the lot and give you a colostomy.'

'That means bringing the gut out on to the stomach and wearing a bag to collect the faeces, doesn't it?' It was stated as a fact, not a question.

David drew in a breath. 'Yes.' He glanced towards Christine. 'Sister will arrange for the stoma nurse to explain what that entails, just in case.' He smiled encouragingly.

'I understand.' The colonel's back became even stiffer. 'Thank you for not dressing it up in frills. I like a blunt man.'

So David had been right. His assessment of the patient had been correct, but that did not excuse his brusqueness with Mrs Turner, thought Holly.

'Perhaps you'll make a cup of tea for Colonel Sanderson,' Christine requested, looking at Holly.

Holly accompanied John Sanderson back to the side-ward and watched as he slumped in his chair.

'I'll fetch that cup of tea,' she said quietly.

His fine blue eyes looked into hers and she could have wept at the courage she saw there. 'Thanks, Staff,' he said in a quiet voice.

What a wonderful old man he was, she thought as she made the tea. It was always difficult for her to distance herself from a patient's anguish. It was all very well being told in training not to become emotionally involved, but it was a different matter when you were on the wards. Even David Quinn with his years of self-control was disturbed at having to tell the colonel his prognosis. She nearly poured boiling water on to her hand, she was so preoccupied with her thoughts, and just moved it in time.

In the side-ward, Holly handed the colonel his tea with a smile. 'Sorry we haven't anything stronger,' she said, hoping her little jest would cheer him.

He smiled his appreciation but didn't speak. She suspected he wanted to be alone so, moving the tray closer to him, said, 'Ring if you want anything,' and closed the door quietly behind her.

Needing to check the treatment book, Holly approached the office. The door was open; David was sitting beside the desk. He looked up as she entered. Light from the window caught half his face, giving the odd impression that it was coloured white and grey. His blue eyes surveyed her steadily. She smiled to acknowledge his presence.

'You seem to get on very well with the colonel,' he said as she pulled the treatment book forward. 'I suppose, in many ways, he's like your father.'

Her fingers tightened on the pencil in her hand. 'Meaning I should have the same rapport with Dad?' She was annoyed to hear how defensive her voice sounded.

'Not necessarily.' His tone was placatory. 'It doesn't always follow.' He shrugged. 'Look at Mike and me, for instance.'

It was the first time she had heard him call his brother Mike. Her tension slipped away and she smiled.

'Thanks,' she said, and meant it, suddenly very happy.

The stern lines of his face softened and he grinned. The corners of his eyes crinkled, the laughter lines about his mouth deepened and his teeth—she only wished hers were so white.

He rose to his feet and looked down at her, his bulk making her feel small and feminine. She liked that.

'I should be the one to thank you for opening my eyes about Mike,' he said, the grin leaving his face, his eyes wistful.

Touched by his admission, she laid a hand on his

arm and was about to murmur words of comfort when——

'Nurse Grant! What are you doing here?' Christine's voice interrupted sharply.

'Staff was about to make me some tea.' David's eyes twinkled at the redhead.

'Er—yes.' Holly said hastily. 'Shall I bring a cup for you, Sister?'

Christine was immaculate, her dress creaseless, every hair in place. 'Yes, please,' she said, but did not smile. 'The auxiliary can make it, though; you get on with your work.' It sounded so hostile.

As Holly went in search of Mrs White she wondered if Christine's coolness was because she was jealous or if the ghost of the previous staff nurse was to blame.

Next evening Holly was off at six. It meant she had to rush home, eat, change and hurry back for the meeting.

'I'll run you in,' her father offered as she passed him a cup of tea. 'I've some books to collect from the library and I'm calling in at the club.' He picked up his teaspoon. 'I could take you home as well if you know what time the meeting will finish.'

He seemed eager to please, and Holly was sorry she had to reply, 'The lift would be great, but I don't know what time it ends.'

'You could phone me at the club,' he suggested.

'Right. I'll do that, then.' She was glad she could please him.

For a moment David's features were superimposed upon her father's. How alike these two men were.

She left him to finish his tea and went to change. Jeans and a white polo-necked jumper were soon slipped on. She pushed her feet into flat beige shoes and took a matching-coloured leather jacket from the wardrobe. Her brown shoulder-bag was lying on the bedroom chair. She flung it on to her shoulder and it bounced on her hip as she ran downstairs.

'Ready, Dad.'

She stood in the doorway of her father's study and watched him heave his tall frame from behind the desk. The ceiling light shone down on his red hair, the harsh electricity deepening the grooves in his face. He seemed more tired than usual and his eyes were wistful, as David's had been. She smiled and kissed his cheek.

'Why don't you stay and have a rest? I can get the bus and collect your books before the meeting starts.'

His smile lifted the sadness from his eyes. 'No—no. It'll do me good to get out.'

Suddenly Holly was grateful to David for this new awareness she felt for her father.

'There's a good film on at the ABC this week,' she said as they drove towards Harrington, and mentioned the title. 'Would you like to see it?'

'Very much.' The eagerness in his voice was a reproach.

'Good, it's a date, then.'

He smiled, and she realised how attractive he must have been as a young man. He was distinguished now, as David would be at her father's age.

He dropped her at the hospital. She made her way to the lecture theatre where the meeting was to be held. When she entered she was surprised to see David'd tall figure—he was talking to Irene.

'Ah, Holly.' The physio beamed at the redhead. 'Meet your partner.' She gestured towards David.

'Partner?'

'Yes. Mr Quinn has offered to help you.' Irene transferred her smile to David. 'He has some pretty good ideas, too.'

'Oh,' Holly said and tried to look pleased, but was

not at all sure she wanted to be paired with David. She could cope in their professional capacity, but now. . . .

David caught hold of her arm. 'Come along, Miss Grant,' he said, using his firm doctor's voice. 'There's no need to be embarrassed.'

He'd read her mind. 'I'm not,' she said, and immediately blushed. He smiled and took her arm. 'You can let go,' she said, annoyed because he was teasing her.

'Oh, I couldn't do that. A gentleman must escort a lady to her seat.' His eyes were twinkling.

'But not like a policeman.' She looked pointedly at the hand on her arm, then laughed up into his face at the ridiculous comparison.

He grinned as he released her. They had reached the table, which was set with paper and pens. Pulling out a seat, he gestured for her to sit. The courtesy pleased her and she said, 'Thanks.'

Chairs scraped as the rest took their seats. A committee was soon formed with the SNO as chairwoman. After an opening address, a lively discussion ensued.

'What about a dance?' 'A raffle's a must. . .' 'I'll see about a jumble sale if you like.'

Then Irene proposed that David and Holly organise the sponsored events. Before Holly could say yea or nay David had agreed for them both.

'I can answer for myself,' she whispered. 'Women do have the vote; you know.'

He smiled. 'So I've heard,' he said. 'Quite a spunky redhead, aren't you?' He was laughing now.

'Looks as if I'll need to be if we're to work together,' she replied smartly.

'Being cheeky again, Staff?' His face assumed a stern expression but his eyes were twinkling.

Their exchange had been spoken in a low tone, but their lack of attention to those around them must have been noticed, for the SNO said, 'Could I have all of your attention, please?' looking at David.

Holly bent her head over her pencil to hide her grin, and felt her leg kicked.

'As everything has been decided I suggest we form our individual groups and start,' the SNO said.

Holly and David were left at the end of the table. She reached down to rub her ankle. 'What are you wearing—boots?' she said, looking sideways at him ruefully.

He drew his chair closer to hers. 'Sorry. But you shouldn't laugh at your consultant.'

'Who—me?' She pointed a finger at herself, her face smooth and innocent, her eyes gleeful.

His hand reached for the paper and pencil. 'I think we'd better get on with our assignment.'

Hearing the formality of his words, she wondered if her familiarity had gone too far. Some of the colour faded from her cheeks and she said, 'By all means,' a little stiffly.

She didn't see the amusement in the glance he cast towards her, because she was writing.

'That's a good little staff nurse,' he said drily.

Her head jerked up. She forgot the difference in their professional status, and was about to say 'You don't need to be so patronising' when she saw the laughter in his eyes and realised he had been teasing. She grinned.

'What about a sponsored walk round the stadium?' he suggested, taking the top off his biro.

'Yes.' She made a note of it, then looked up at him. 'A sponsored swim might be a good idea.'

'Yes.' He gave a wide smile and his eyes travelled over her figure, making her wish she had not made that suggestion. She had discarded her jacket, and the jumper she wore outlined her bust rather too well. 'I'd like to see you in a swim-suit, or do you wear a bikini?' He was altogether too interested.

It was her turn to give him a kick. 'I suggest you keep your mind on what you're doing, Doctor,' she said, blushing.

'But I am,' he said, laughing.

'Hmm.' She smiled. Hot blood runs in your veins, of that I'm quite sure, she thought. Her face brightened. Perhaps he doesn't swim. But, looking at his broad back and glancing at the firm thighs outlined by his trousers, she knew he did. Ah—but he was a consultant. Surely it would not do for him to appear half-naked in front of the hospital staff? She smiled and said hopefully, 'I don't suppose you'll put yourself up for sponsorship?'

A mischievous gleam crept into his eyes. 'Of course I will. I mean to make the whole hospital pay to see me in a swimsuit. I'm sure I'll raise a lot of money.' And he laughed.

Heads turned in their direction. A vision of him in bathing trunks rose in Holly's mind and she busied herself in writing to hide her blush.

'Will you sponsor me?' he asked, and the way he said it made her think that he knew what she had been thinking.

Her blush spread to her neck and she waited, for a moment, for it to subside before answering, 'I might manage five pence,' keeping her face straight, though her eyes betrayed her; they were dancing.

He laughed. 'In spite of the fact that you've cut me to the quick with that offer, I'm prepared to sponsor you five pounds a length.' His eyes softened. 'See how highly I value you?'

Her breathing quickened, and she felt herself leaning towards him—drawn by a sudden longing.

'Holly. . .' he began, his voice gentle.

'I hope you two are working hard.' Irene's voice came from behind them, her tone accusing.

The red and dark heads swung towards her, Holly's curls brushing his face. 'Of course we are,' they answered in unison, and laughed.

'We—ell?' Holly saw envy below the doubt in the physio's eyes.

'We've thought up some great ideas, really we have,' Holly assured her.

'Well. . .' Irene shrugged. 'Oh, all right, then,' she said, and left them.

They turned back to the table, the physio already forgotten.

'What about a marathon dance?' David suggested.

'That's a bit ambitious,' Holly said.

'Should be fun, though.' He grinned. 'Will you be my partner?' It sounded like a challenge.

'If you like.' Her tone was offhand and she bent to write again. She didn't want him to see how pleased she was he had asked her.

'Oh, I *do* like,' he replied.

She glanced up at him then, and could not decide if he was teasing her or not. He looked amused, and yet. . .there was something behind the twinkle in his eyes. Perhaps it was the emphasis he'd placed in the 'do'.

Their attention was distracted by the noise of chairs scraping on the wooden floor as the others prepared to leave.

'I think we should meet in a fortnight's time.' The SNO's voice cut clearly through the shuffling. There were murmurs of assent, and the meeting broke up.

'Can I give you a lift?' David offered.

Holly was bundling papers into her bag. 'No, thanks.' She glanced up at his enquiring face. 'My father's taking me home.'

'I'd like a word with him, so I'll wait with you until he comes.' He smiled down at her. 'That is if you can bear my company for a bit longer.;'

She wanted him to stay and yet she didn't. She wanted him to go because he disturbed her and, for the same reason, she wanted him to stay.

'I was to phone him at the club when the meeting finished,' she explained. 'I don't want to keep you.'

Perhaps he would go now. Holly was trying to put on her jacket without putting down her bag. He took it from her, slung it over his shoulder and helped untangle her sleeves.

'Thanks,' she said, feeling like a gawky schoolgirl.

He handed back her bag. 'You don't need to phone him; I'll run you to the club.'

Again she thanked him. What else could she do?

His car was parked near by. As they drove the short distance, he said, 'Mr Grant's a difficult man to get hold of, he's so busy.'

She murmured an affirmative.

'I'm thinking of buying a house.'

His words were so unexpected that they jolted her. Was he thinking of getting married? Was his relationship with Christine as serious as that?

The happiness of the evening was swept away. His words suddenly showed her how much her emotions had really been stirred by this man; they brought Christine into the car. She was glad when he drew up outside the Victorian façade of the club.

The porter acknowledged David as they entered, greeting him by name. Then, turning to Holly, the grey-haired man said, 'Your father told me to expect you, miss. I'll phone the lounge and let him know you're here.'

They waited, surrounded by another era. A massive carved wooden staircase swept up to the floor above, carpeted in thick red Wilton. A polished brown leather settee glowed in the shadows of the hall.

Her father appeared almost immediately. His similarity to David impressed her once more, especially when they stood facing each other. It was like meeting like. She felt the force of their integrity, the power which emanated from them both.

Holly had been so busy with her thoughts that she caught only the end of their conversation. Her father was saying, 'Why don't you come to the house now?'

'I'd be delighted,' said David.

'Don't you think it's a bit late?' Holly protested.

Mr Grant looked at his watch. 'It's only nine-thirty.'

'Early yet,' David agreed.

Holly watched David's headlights following them. She could see the dark bulk of his figure behind the wheel.

When they entered the house her father said, 'Would you make some coffee, Holly?'

She was only too eager to comply and used ground coffee deliberately, to delay her return to the lounge. When it was ready she carried the tray through. Warmth rushed to greet her as she opened the door; her father had lit the fire, sending shadows to mix with those shed by the table lamps.

'What a comfortable room,' David said as Holly placed the tray on the coffee-table. She thought she detected a trace of envy in his voice as he added, 'It's so welcoming.'

'My wife was responsible for that.' Holly's father glanced affectionately at the photo of a pretty woman, a younger version of Holly, on the mantelpiece. 'She was a great home-maker.'

Holly knew her father had loved her mother, but it was only now that she realised how deeply. Was it because of her new awareness of him, or was it because she was falling in love with David?

Her hand shook as she poured the coffee and a little spilt in the saucer. Love. How had that thought popped into her head? Just because she found David attractive sexually didn't mean that she was in love with him. She was sure many of her colleagues at Harrington General were equally aware of his maleness.

Holly was sitting on the couch. David was in the armchair she always thought of as her mother's. Rising, she handed him his cup, and as he took it from her their eyes met, and a warmth that had nothing to do with the fire spread through her whole body. She felt as if sunlight were bathing her, caressing her, soothing her with gentle hands. Her breath caught in her throat. She had never experienced anything like it. It was as if she were looking into blue skies that stretched forever, where there was no pain or sorrow, only delight.

'Am I to get a cup?' Her father's voice came from behind her.

The feeling had only lasted a moment but seemed an eternity. She felt as if she was returning from a far place and wondered if David had sensed it also. There was a seriousness about his face and eyes, but otherwise she could detect nothing.

Holly returned to her seat and poured coffee for her father. After handing it to him she said, 'If you'll excuse me I'll leave you two together.'

Sleep was evasive that night. She tried lying very still, but it didn't help; she kept seeing David's face every time she closed her eyes. It must have been past two o'clock before she fell into an exhausted sleep.

The following day she was giving Colonel Sanderson his pre-med. 'I've got my fingers crossed,' she said, smiling.

He sighed. 'You know, Staff, in all the years of my

army career I've never had to face such a challenge.' His eyes were clear, and her admiration for him increased. She was flattered that he had confided in her.

'I'm sure it will be your greatest victory,' she said with a confidence that wasn't feigned.

He smiled affectionately at her. 'You've been a great comfort to me. I envy the man you marry.'

She blushed and left him to rest.

Janet Roberts was to take the colonel to Theatre. Holly intercepted her wheeling the trolley into the side-ward.

'I'll take the Colonel to Theatre,' she said, reaching for the notes.

'Sister won't like that,' Janet said in consternation.

'Sister won't know,' whispered Holly. 'I'll be back before she knows I've gone.'

'Well?' Worry lines appeared on the third-year's forehead.

They helped the sleepy patient on to the trolley and pushed it through the door. The theatres were close by. It was worth the slight anxiety when the colonel whispered through dry lips. 'Thanks for coming with me,' before she left him with the anaesthetist.

Ten minutes later she was about to enter the ward when Christine called her to the office.

'Come in and close the door,' she said with icy politeness, and, when Holly obeyed, continued, 'Why did you take the colonel to Theatre?' Christine's face was stiff with suppressed anger.

Holly moistened her dry lips. 'I knew he would like me to.'

'Really.' The sarcasm was thick. 'Do you usually disobey the ward sister?'

Holly thought she detected disillusion in the blue eyes turned to hers, and her heart sank.

'I cannot tolerate disobedience in a nurse,' Christine said sternly. 'And I'm disappointed in you. I was beginnning to think you would make a good staff nurse.' She frowned. 'I'm debating whether to put this lapse on your report, but it wouldn't look good, would it?'

Holly's face was expressionless, concealing her dismay. It certainly wouldn't, she thought.

'I'm sorry, Sister,' she said, and meant it. Christine was right. Discipline was an essential quality in a nurse. She hoped the regret she was feeling was reflected in her eyes. It must have been, for she saw Christine's face soften.

'I'll let you off this time,' she said.

'Thank you, Sister.' Holly's gratitude was evident.

Every time the phone rang that morning Holly hurried to answer it, hoping to hear the colonel was returning to the ward.

When eventually he did arrive she was busy aspirating a patient who had had a partial gastrectomy earlier and could not leave him immediately.

As soon as she had finished she hurried to the sideward. David Quinn, still in Theatre greens, was standing beside the bed with Christine.

A Ryle's tube was strapped to John Sanderson's pale cheek, and an intravenous infusion was in place. He was awake but drowsy.

'John. Can you hear me?' David spoke clearly, leaning over the patient.

Glazed eyes moved slowly in the direction of the voice. 'Yes,' was whispered from the dry lips.

'It's good news. We managed to remove the tumour. It wasn't necesssary to give you a colostomy.'

The patient's murmured, 'Thank God,' was heard by them all.

Holly felt tears sting her eyes as she turned to go.

She had heard what she wanted. Her hand was on the door-handle when Christine said, 'I'd like you to special the colonel for now, Staff.'

Holly moved closer to the bed, grateful that the rising tears had subsided. David did not seem to notice her as he left with Christine. Holly was sure it was because he was still thinking about the colonel and that he was not snubbing her.

The touch of her fingers on his wrist roused John, and he smiled. 'Staff,' he whispered.

'Don't try to speak,' Holly said, her tone gentle, a smile in her eyes.

He frowned. 'Did I hear David telling me. . .?' His hand moved in slow motion towards his stomach.

Holly caught it in hers. 'Yes.' Delight for him filled her voice with lightness.

The taut lines on his face softened. He looked years younger. 'Thank you,' he murmured. 'And will you thank David for me?'

'Of course.'

His head, which he had raised slightly, fell back on the pillow.

Holly took his blood-pressure, aspirated his Ryle's tube, checked that the infusion was running properly and that the needle was secure. Lifting the bedcovers she inspected his dressing for signs of bleeding. Holly reached behind his locker for his face cloth, rinsed it in the sink and bathed his face. She checked the drawer sheet was uncrumpled, the bedclothes not too tight over his toes, and had just placed the bell within reach of his hand when Anne Wilson, the second-year nurse, came in.

'Sister sent me to special the colonel,' she said. 'Thought it was time for me to take more responsibility.'

Holly looked at the rosy-cheeked round face, detecting anxiety in the blue eyes, and thought how Anne would look more at home on the farm from which she came than on a hospital ward. She knew, though, that Anne's anxiety came from her caring attitude—the girl was frightened of making a mistake.

Holly smiled encouragingly, and handed over. 'Don't worry. You'll be fine, and I'll look in from time to time.' She pointed to the bell. 'Ring if you're worried.'

'Thanks, Staff.' The young nurse looked with envy at Holly. 'I wish I could be like you—confident.'

'It'll come. You'll see.'

The ward was very busy. Sister was supposed to be off duty at six, but she lingered, annoying Holly with her presence. Doesn't trust me, I suppose, she thought.

Christine was still there an hour later. Holly was checking the post-operative patients when Johnny Simpson, the house surgeon, looked in just as the visitors were arriving.

'I see the "ice maiden"——' using Sister Nicol's nickname '—is still here,' he whispered as he looked at the colonel's charts. 'Keeping tabs on you, is she?' He smiled.

Holly grimaced but made no reply. He looked very tired. 'Why don't you slip into the kitchen? I'll ask Nurse Bailey to make you a cup of tea.'

'Thanks, Holly.' His smiled broadened. 'But I'm just going for supper.'

At eight o'clock the visitors had just left and Holly was checking Mr Taylor's dressing—he had had a ligation of varicose veins—when she noticed Christine standing beside Mr Wilson's bed; he was a patient who had been admitted as an emergency appendicectomy the previous day.

What on earth's she doing? Holly frowned. Christine

glanced in her direction and beckoned. A feeling of apprehension gripped Holly. Something was wrong.

'Send for Mr Simpson now, please,' Christine said, placing the emphasis on the 'now'. There was a calm certainty about her voice, and she was reaching for the oxygen.

The patient was very pale, cyanotic, breathless and anxious. Holly thought he must have had a heart attack, but as she was about to hurry away Christine caught her arm and said in a low voice, 'Tell him I think Mr Wilson has had a pulmonary embolus.'

Holly left Christine drawing the curtains round the bed, and heard her say, 'You're going to be fine, Mr Wilson. Just take this oxygen,' as she placed the mask over his face. 'Doctor will be here in a moment to look at you.' Her voice was calm, soothing.

A great feeling of relief mixed with despair swept over Holly as she realised that everything would be all right. The experienced ward sister had recognised Mr Wilson symptoms, which she, Holly, had missed because she had been concentrating on today's operations. She had heard Mr Wilson say, before Christine had put the mask over his face, 'I didn't like to bother anyone about the pain in my chest; they were all so busy.'

After phoning Johnny, Holly hurried back, hot and flustered, filled with anxiety.

'Fetch the sphygmo and some charts, will you?' Christine requested, her fingers on Mr Wilson's pulse.

Holly felt even worse. She should have thought to bring them herself. Johnny caught up with her on the way back down the ward with the blood-pressure apparatus under her arm.

'Bet you're glad Sister's here.' He winked at her.

'Yes. Very.' It was a heartfelt reply.

Christine sent her off again to collect the syringe

tray; the doctor would give an anticoagulant to dissolve the clot.

It was late when Christine and Holly left that evening. The report had been given, and normality had returned to the ward. Mr Wilson had improved and an extra night nurse had arrived to special him.

They walked down the corridor together. Christine was as immaculate as ever, while Holly was hot and sticky, her hair in wisps about her neck.

Holly expected Christine to reprimand her for not being aware of Mr Wilson's condition, and found herself tensing in expectation, but all Christine said was, 'I knew something was wrong—that's why I stayed.' She smiled at Holly with understanding. 'It wasn't because I didn't think you capable, but because of. . .' she frowned, trying to find the right words '. . .a sixth sense, I suppose you'd call it. You'll find you'll develop it in time and with experience.'

Holly could see now why David held Christine in such esteem. She was a dedicated professional who had achieved that fine balance of caring without becoming too emotionally involved.

The corridor light shone full upon the pale face, accentuating the fine lines beside the eyes and mouth, lines that had not appeared on Holly's. What a long way I have to go before I am as good as my ward sister, she thought, thrilled that Christine had treated her like an able colleague.

As they parted on the hospital steps, Christine smiled, and it was a genuine smile, free from suspicion. This was no 'ice maiden' but a warm-hearted woman. No doubt David had found this out already.

On the bus home, Holly watched as its lights made disjointed darts in the dark. A picture of David Quinn in Theatre greens leaning over the colonel, the clear lines of his face sharpened and intense, flashed on to the window. Sadness deepened the green of her eyes. What chance did she have of creeping into David's heart—young, well built, bursting with health and vitality, compared with the slender, willowy, ethereal quality of the sophisticated Christine?

CHAPTER FIVE

HOLLY had not seen Angie for a while. Her friend had gone away for her nights off, and when she'd came back their duties had not coincided.

Coming on duty next day, Angie caught up with her in the corridor. 'My duty's been changed and I'm off at one.' She looked rested; the dark smudges below her eyes had lifted.

Holly's face brightened. 'Great. So am I.'

'How about coming to my room for a chat?' suggested Angie.

'I'd love to.'

'See you in the canteen, then.'

The morning passed quickly. Christine's changed attitude was noticed by the nurses.

'What have you done to get into Sister's good books?' asked Janet Roberts, a trace of envy in her voice.

Holly just smiled and shrugged.

When she came off at one she was very tired. The strain of yesterday was catching up with her and she felt drained.

A plate of fish and chips was practically eaten by the time Angie joined her. Holly looked up apologetically,

'Sorry, couldn't wait. I was so ravenous.'

'That's OK.' Angie placed a bowl of soup with an apple and roll down on the table and took the chair opposite.

'Is that all you're having?' Holly viewed her friend's choice with amazement.

'I'm trying to lose weight.' Angie smiled. 'Too many chocolate biscuits on night duty.'

When they had finished, Angie suggested coffee in her room. The nurses' home was at the back of the hospital, overlooking the park. The trees were dressed in their fresh spring clothes, the green leaves clean and free from pollution. Angie's room was at the top of the four-storeyed building.

'How d'you like Women's Surgical?' Holly asked, sitting on tbe bed and slipping off her shoes.

Angie was filling the electric kettle. 'It's great. Sister Blake's wonderful to work with.'

'So I've heard,' said Holly, and before yesterday she would have envied her friend, but not now. She knew Christine Nicol was the better ward sister.

'And, of course, David's the ward consultant.'

Holly heard the admiration in her friend's voice. 'He's very professional, I'll grant you that. Very good at his job, but a bit ruthless,' she added, remembering his heartlessness towards Mrs Turner.

Angie switched on the kettle. 'I don't agree.'

Holly was surprised at the vehemence with which she said it. 'You're just saying that because he's Mike's brother,' she said.

'No, I'm not.' Angie spooned coffee into two mugs. 'One of our patients, a Mrs Turner, in for a mastectomy, told me how he went out of his way to help her.' She poured the boiled water on to the granules and added milk. 'Apparently she had arrived late for her Out-patients' appointment. . .' Angie passed Holly her coffee '. . .because she had arranged for someone to visit to advise on financial matters and then. . .' here Angie's face assumed the 'so there' expression '. . .he insisted in running her home himself.'

'Did he?' said Holly in a faint voice.

'Yes,' Angie replied, pleased with her response.

'And that's not all. Sister Blake told us it isn't the first time David has shown such kindness,' she said.

Holly drank her coffee, feeling small and mean. She should not have judged David. To change the subject she said, 'How's Mike?'

Happiness transformed Angie's face. 'Fine. We're getting engaged.' Her eyes slid shyly from the redhead's.

Holly jumped up, almost upsetting her mug and just saving it in time. She rushed over to her friend and gave her a hug. 'That's marvellous!' Though she didn't envy Angie. Mike was too—she thought for a moment—young for her. She was herself not old, but she had been more mature two years ago when she'd attained her majority.

Holly had just left Angie's and was walking across the hospital grounds when she saw David striding towards her.

'Ah, Holly. I was looking for you.'

Her first thought was that Christine had told him how Holly had missed Mr Wilson's symptoms, so she viewed him with caution.

When he said, 'What are you doing this evening?' she was taken by surprise and stammered.

'N—nothing,' and was annoyed to see amusement spring into his eyes as she blushed.

He linked his arm in hers and walked with her.

'Don't do that!' she exclaimed, pulling away. 'You know what the hospital grapevine's like.'

His grip tightened and he grinned. Two nurses were approaching and Holly was sure he was doing it out of devilment. His taking her arm in such an intimate fashion would be all over the hospital in minutes.

'Don't you want your name linked with mine?' he said in a reproachful tone, though his grin was cheeky.

She had to smile. 'You are a devil disguised as a doctor,' she said.

He laughed. 'I was wondering if you could bear the company of this devil doctor this evening. I thought we could discuss more events to sponsor over dinner.'

They had reached the main gate and had paused. He was wearing a grey suit, and a white shirt with a red and silver striped tie. No matter how she tried to suppress her traitorous heart, it would beat faster. She had sought to find faults in his character and his attitude towards Mike, but he had shown her that her own behaviour to her father needed attention. She had hung on to his unkindness towards Mrs Turner, but Angie had disproved that. She felt defenceless now, vulnerable, almost naked, and she drew her trench coat tighter about her.

'All right,' she said as lightly as possible, staring him boldly in the eye. 'As long as it's a working dinner.'

He was looking past her, over her shoulder. His face had lost its easy, relaxed expression. 'Whatever did you think I had in mind, Miss Grant?' He was her ward consultant. 'I'll collect you at eight. Sister Nicol told me you were off then.'

A figure in blue jeans appeared in the corner of her eye. She turned her head. It was Andrew.

'Hi, Holly,' he said, his pleasant smile including David. 'Are you going for the bus?'

The stiffness of David's figure did not relax. He nodded to the younger man and left them without speaking.

You don't have to be so stuffy, Holly thought, watching his tall figure stride away, his back as straight as the colonel's.

She felt thwarted somehow. He was such a difficult man to understand. One minute he showed he was attracted to her, the next he was using his status to distance himself. Why? It must be Christine, she decided as she walked with Andrew to the bus-stop.

'Hey, Holly!'

She had almost forgotten he was there, so involved she was with her thoughts of the consultant.

'Sorry, Andrew.' She linked her arm in his. He was so uncomplicated and restful. 'I am going for the bus.'

'I'll wait with you. My bus goes from the same stop.'

That evening she was ready before time. She didn't know where David would take her, but assumed it would be somewhere sophisticated. So she chose a fine cream jersey silk dress with a high collar, bat-sleeves and a full skirt. Beige shoes, matching bag and a jacket of a deeper shade would complete the outfit.

Facing the mirror, she wondered why she was taking so much trouble and wished she was meeting Andrew. She brushed her bouncing curls, trying to tame them, but was unsuccessful; they seemed to have a life of their own.

She frowned. Her dress looked all right but her hairstyle was too unsophisticated. She swept the red tresses up and, reaching for some combs, fixed them in place.

'That's better. I look five years older,' she told her reflection.

Holly hardly ever used make-up, but tonight she decided that a light dusting of powder might subdue her rosy cheeks, a pale lipstick lighten her red lips.

When she joined her father in the lounge he looked up from his paper and said, 'You're looking very smart. More like your mother every day.'

Spontaneously she bent and kissed him. 'Thanks. You're a great morale-booster.'

He seemed pleased with her reply. 'Who's the lucky fellow?'

She laid her coat and bag on the couch. 'David Quinn.'

'Oh?' It was a very expressive 'oh'.

She felt she had to explain—he was looking too interested. 'He's taking me out to a working dinner. We're going to discuss more events to sponsor.'

'Are those classed as working clothes?'

Holly could see he was suppressing his laughter. 'Yes,' she answered shortly. Then to take the sting out of her abruptness and to prevent further teasing she said, 'I've left your dinner ready; you only have to pop it in the microwave.'

The big hand on the clock was just moving to the twelve when the bell rang.

'Punctual,' said her father, rising to help her on with her coat. 'That's a good sign.'

'Really, Dad.' She laughed up into his face, its shape so like David's.

'Have a good time.' He bent and kissed her cheek.

David's eyes gleamed with appreciation when she opened the door, but hers grew round with dismay. He was wearing blue jeans, matching shirt and denim jacket—admittedly designer-made, but casual. . .very casual.

Seeing the expression on her face, he said, 'You look great, but I thought a working dinner would be more practical in an informal atmosphere.'

He's trying to save my face, she thought and wanted to curl up with embarrassment. What must he be thinking? That she had expected it to be a real date? How awful. Then she took a deep breath and said, It'll only take me a moment to change.' She was closing the door as she spoke, in her confusion.

'Take as much time as you like,' he was calling through the almost closed door. 'I don't want to disturb your father.'

It's not him you're disturbing, Holly thought as she rushed upstairs. It's me.

In her bedroom, she paused to catch her breath. Then, throwing off her clothes she bathed her burning face in cold water, reached in the wardrobe for her jeans and pulled them on. Yanking at the dressing-table drawer to pick a sweater, she nearly pulled it out altogether and had to struggle with it to push it back. Damn that man. She gave it a kick and it slid into place. I wish I could slide him into place so easily.

Slipping on a pink sweater, she hoped it would not make her hotter than she already was. She had to grope for her brown flatties which had been kicked to the back, under the bed. Catching up her leather jacket and bag, she rushed for the stairs.

'Thought you'd gone,' called her father from the lounge.

'Just forgot something,' she replied. My head, she thought, and prayed he would not come into the hall.

David put aside what appeared to be a medical journal, leapt out of the car and came round to open the passenger-door for her. 'That was quick.' There was an underlying tension in the lightly spoken words.

Holly took her seat and dumped her jacket and bag in her lap. He sat beside her and she expected him to start the engine, but he was looking at her hair.

Suddenly he reached forward, startling her so that she jerked away. He laughed.

'Not frightened of me, are you?' His eyes were laughing.

'No, of course not.'

'In that case. . .' He reached towards her again. This time she remained still. What was he going to do? 'I prefer you with your hair down,' he said, taking the combs out, releasing the red curls so that they tumbled about her shoulders.

Disappointment caught at her throat, making her speechless. She had thought he was going to kiss her. Then she blushed. There had been something intimate about the gesture. It was the sort of thing a lover would do, and she supposed David had had plenty of practice releasing Christine's blonde tresses. Holly was shocked at the jealous force which gripped her.

'You're too young to wear your hair like that,' he said, starting the engine.

'Yes, Father,' she said without thinking, and gasped.

But he laughed. It broke the embarrassing tension between them.

To prove to him that she was not a child or a teenager, but an adult, she said, 'What about sponsoring a quick-change event?'

'Oh, no.' He grinned. 'That wouldn't be fair. You would win every time and cost the sponsors a fortune.

It was her turn to laugh.

'I thought we'd go to. . .' He named a popular pub which had a good restaurant attached.

When they reached it they had difficulty finding a parking space big enough for the Rover. David's face was tense, his hands clenched on the wheel.

'I think we'll have to park somewhere else,' he was saying, when two young couples came out of the pub, climbed into a Mini and a Metro and drove away, leaving enough space for David's car. He relaxed; even his denim jacket slackened across his back.

As they left the car he took her elbow, and his closeness filled her with a longing so fierce that she stumbled.

'Good job I had hold of your arm,' he said, laughter in his voice.

'I've booked a table, so we can choose our menu and have a drink while we wait.' He glanced down at her. 'You do drink?'

'Yes.' She gave him a look that spoke more than words. 'I've even passed my twenty-first birthday.'

He smiled. 'D'you have an age complex?'

Looking pointedly at the clothes he was wearing, she said, 'No. Have you?' and wished she hadn't when she saw his face tighten and heard him say,

'You do have a habit of speaking frankly, don't you?' He was annoyed, but not with her. He had dressed to fit in with her generation. It was a long time since he had felt so foolish.

'What would you like to drink?' he said and smiled, and was rewarded by seeing Holly's face lose its stiffness.

'Sherry, please.'

'Two or three,' he said grinning. 'Slight inebriation might improve our brain-power.'

Suddenly she was very happy and laughed. 'But I don't think we'd get much work done.'

Holly watched his broad back move easily to the front of the crowded bar. His height commanded attention and he was served quickly.

David had the menu between his teeth when he came back, a drink in each hand.

'You must be hungry,' she quipped, taking it from his mouth, and he laughed.

They decided on their preferences and David returned to the bar to order. Seated once more beside her, he raised his glass, 'Cheers. Here's to a successful working dinner.'

She took a sip of sherry; it caught on the back of her throat, bringing on a coughing fit. As he patted her back he said, grinning, 'Are you sure you drink?'

Holly glared between coughs. He raised his hands and said, 'Sorry,' but his grin broadened.

They were called for their meal and went into the restaurant.

'What about a sponsored cycle-ride?' he suggested, a spoon of soup halfway to his mouth.

Holly broke a piece off her bread. 'That's a good idea. We could use the moors.'

'We'd need people at various points to render first aid, if it became necessary.'

She drank some soup. 'I could supervise that,' she said, dipping her spoon in the bowl. 'I'm sure there'll be quite a few nurses who will volunteer.'

'Won't you be one of the contestants?' He sounded disappointed. 'I'm sure you'd look great in shorts.'

'So would Sister Nicol—her legs are perfect.'

'I know.' He smiled. 'I'll ask her.'

There it was again—an intimate knowledge of Christine.

'What about sponsoring a goat-count?' she suggested to lead the conversation in another direction, employing facetiousness to cover her misery.

He laughed. 'Or a postman-count?'

'A bus-count?'

'A baby-count?'

Each vied with the other in suggesting more and more outrageous ideas, and the more she watched the expressions chase each other across his face, the more drawn to him she became. And when he said, 'What about. . .?' and whispered something even more ridiculous, she laughed until the tears fell.

The other diners looked in their direction. One of them rose and came towards the table. It was Andrew. She was wiping her eyes when he said, 'So this is where your working dinner is.' He glanced at David, who had risen. 'Holly told me she was meeting you.' The way he said it made it sound as if he were a serious boyfriend.

Holly was annoyed. They were only friends, and she was surprised at Andrew's deviousness. She had thought he was such an open person. He was a head shorter than David, but just as broad. He was also dressed casually, but his denims sat more easily on his stocky frame. His smooth face lacked David's maturity.

Andrew must have seen her dismay, for he bent close to her ear and whispered, '"All's fair in love and war".'

She moved her head away but knew it must have looked as if he had said something intimate, and this annoyed her afresh while at the same time it surprised her. She hadn't realised he was so fond of her.

Andrew gestured towards a grey-haired man sitting at his vacated table. 'I'm here with my father.'

Holly caught David looking at Andrew and herself. His face was solemn and unreadable.

'Holly told me about the efforts you are all making to raise money for a scanner. Can I help?' He brushed a lock of hair from his forehead. It must have seemed a very young gesture to David, watching them. But then they *were* young and he must remember that.

'We need volunteers,' said David, and Holly thought his tone stiff.

Andrew looked at her. 'If I help you will you help me?' He grinned.

'How?'

His face straightened. 'You know how the vet school's threatened with closure?' When she nodded he continued, 'Well, we're planning a demonstration—placards and a petition—outside the school.' His expression became earnest. 'It's ridiculous, really, in a farming area like this, to transfer the students to London.'

'I suppose the powers that be will have taken that into consideration,' David said in his consultant-to-student voice.

'It's easy to see you're no farmer,' Andrew said, his eyes angry.

'True,' said David. 'But I do know that important decisions are not made lightly.'

Holly suspected he was referring to those he had to make for the patients in his care. She turned to Andrew.

'I'll help if I can. What d'you want me to do?' She forgot her annoyance with him.

'I think it's time we were leaving.' Andrew's father had joined them, unobserved.

After introducing him, Andrew said to Holly, 'I'll phone you tomorrow and fill you in.'

'Time for us to go as well.' David signalled for the bill.

Outside, the air was cooler and Holly was glad she had brought her jacket.

There was a coolness about David, also, as they drove home, a subtle difference; the camaraderie had gone. Had Andrew come between them? She could have told him the truth about the younger man, but why should she? David was not interested in her, except as a diversion.

'I suppose you know what you're doing?'

His words jolted her from the misery of her thoughts. 'Doing?' Her tone was puzzled. Was he talking about Andrew?

'Yes.' His tone was impatient. 'The hospital authorities might not like one of their nurses parading with a placard. You brought yourself to their attention once before when you supported the junior doctors in their campaign for shorter hours.'

Immediately she was angry, glad to have something to vent her disappointed emotions on. 'What I do with my off duty has nothing to do with them.' She glanced sideways at him. 'Or with you.' His profile was immobile. 'I don't recall hearing that you offered your support.'

He didn't answer; he just turned to face her and his expression made her feel small. She knew his silence was more eloquent than words. It was as if he had said 'Not all of us need to carry banners.' He must have done something more positive than she to reduce the junior doctors' hours.

As he turned on the engine and put the car into gear, he said, 'Be careful. It wouldn't do for us to lose our new staff nurse.'

So his concern was for the ward, not for her, she thought as they drove out of the car park.

CHAPTER SIX

HOLLY did not have a minute to herself over the next two weeks. The ward was very busy, and her off duty was occupied in organising her nursing friends either to sponsor or to take part in the events.

Christine's day off fell on the day of the marathon dance. When the ward round was finished the day before David said to the registrar and houseman, 'You go ahead to the other ward; I just want a word with Staff.'

His attitude towards Holly had been coolly professional since their working dinner. It had allowed her emotions to settle.

'Would you like some coffee?' she asked politely, thinking he wanted to discuss a patient.

'No, thanks,' he said just as politely. 'Just wanted to tell you I won't be able to partner you to the dance.'

Holly was relieved. She had been worrying about the hours she would have had to spend in his arms, and had been trying to think of a way to excuse herself.

The early June sunlight fell directly upon him. His white coat was spotless; his hair had recently been cut close to his head, making his face seem leaner and paler; dark smudges below his eyes looked as if his cheeks had been touched with a sooty thumb. He had lost weight as well, and this caused worry to niggle and knot inside her. Was he ill?

'You look very tired,' she blurted out, unable to contain her concern.

He smiled. It was the first time his face had relaxed

in her presence since their meal. 'Too many late nights, I expect.'

For a moment she believed him and envied Christine, but the strain in his eyes and the tenseness of his body made her think it was more than that. He was overworking.

'Are you sure I can't make you a coffee?' she asked gently.

'No, thanks.' His face softened. 'I've a round to do over the way, and a hundred and one other things to do as well.' He paused in the doorway. 'I hope you'll find another partner.'

'Oh, yes.' She shrugged. 'Andrew will be delighted to fill in.'

She looked so fresh and bright, her intelligent face crowned with copper curls. He sighed, and his shoulders sagged a little. 'Good.' He stared at the floor, then raised his head and looked at her. 'I wish. . .' He waved a hand. 'No matter,' and he left her wondering what it was he had wished.

Holly did not see him for a week and heard he was in London at a conference. Christine was off at the weekend and it was rumoured that she, also, was in the capital.

David appeared the day before the sponsored swim and Holly wondered if he would take part. She only caught a flash of his white coat as he hurried in and out of the ward, so she couldn't ask him.

Her day off did not coincide with the swim. She was supposed to finish at six but a car crash delayed her. Two admissions in Theatre took longer than was expected, and she stayed on to special the abdominal injury until a spare nurse was available.

Having been so busy, she had missed her tea but decided not to stop and eat as it would be too close to her swim and it would have made her even later.

Holly was crossing the hospital forecourt when she saw David about to climb into his car. At the same time he saw her.

'Hello,' he said, smiling. How she had missed that smile. 'I expect the emergency made you late as well. Would you like a lift to the pool?'

He had put on weight, and a light tan made him look even more handsome. She was so glad to see him that she could have hugged him, and felt lost because she had to restrain herself.

'Yes, please.' She could not say more. The sight of him was like a pain, making her speechless.

'Hop in,' he said, opening the passenger-door.

Her awareness of him was so great that even her nerve-endings seemed to be alive. Swallowing, she said with an effort, hoping she sounded bright and bubbly, 'The marathon dance was a success.'

The smile left his face. 'So I've heard.'

He sounded grim, and she wondered why. As he drove through the quietened streets she thought back to that evening. It had been very tiring and she had had to lean on Andrew quite a bit, relying on his strength to hold her up. Surely David could not be referring to that?

To break the tension she said, 'Was your conference a success?'

'The hospital grapevine's been at it again, I see.' His tone was sarcastic.

'Yes, it has.' She added boldly, 'So, was it?'

He smiled. 'I like your spirit, Holly, and, as a matter of fact, it was—a great success. It was an AIDS symposium.'

Immediately she was interested and would have questioned him further, but he was parking the car at the pool.

There was a festive air about the place when they

went in, almost as if a gala were taking place. A cheer greeted their appearance.

'We thought you'd chickened out!' '. . .thought better of it.' '. . .found something better to do.' Comments flew at them along with some curious glances, which Holly ignored.

She left David and went to change. When she came out the pool was empty. David was standing in neatly fitting black swimming trunks, waiting for her. His physique was impressive; broad of shoulder, slim of hips, legs a woman would have envied—not too muscular—and the hair on his chest was not too thick, nor too thin; just right, she decided.

Holly had bought a one-piece swimsuit; she wasn't going to be ogled. Its black colour, purchased to conceal her curves, did the opposite, emphasising her thirty-six-inch bust.

David's eyes opened a fraction wider.

'I didn't know we were to be the star attraction,' she said as she joined him and wished she could hide her blush.

'You're taking it very well,' he said, smiling with approval.

She grinned, keeping her eyes on his face because the closeness of his near-naked body was making her truant mind wonder what it would be like to touch and be touched by him. Her skin became hot and she was glad when he gestured towards the pool.

'Shall we?'

They dived together. The shock of the water made her gasp, and she swallowed some of it. Her sponsor was for ten lengths. When she came up for air she could see David cleaving the water well ahead of her.

Finishing her ninth, she paused at the top of the pool. David was standing at the bottom, already finished.

'Not giving up now, are you?' he called, joined by a chorus of the spectators.

Holly was a good swimmer, but exhausted and cold; her tiring day and lack of food were catching up with her. When she stayed where she was the catcalls started, and she knew she would have to continue.

She was halfway down the pool when a buzzing in her ears and spots before her eyes caused her to flounder. Vaguely she heard a splash and felt strong arms haul her to the side. She was hoisted out of the water by waiting hands.

When she opened her eyes, the first thing she saw was David's anxious face bending over her; drops of water clung to his skin like raindrops, and his wet hair, flattened to his skull, altered the shape of his head so that she did not recognise him immediately. It was his voice saying, 'You gave us quite a fright,' that cleared her vision.

He gave rapid orders and she felt herself lifted again. Holly knew it was David's arms that held her so gently when he said, 'You'll be all right in a moment.'

Someone must have laid a rug on one of the benches, for she felt it prickle when she was laid upon it. Taking a towel from eager hands, he rubbed her vigorously.

Hysteria rose within her. This wasn't how she had envisioned the touch of his hands. She protested, 'I can do that,' but her voice was feeble and her limbs felt heavy. She could hardly raise her hand.

When she was dry he tightened the blanket about her.

'Drink this,' his voice commanded as he supported her against him.

Holly swallowed the hot sweet tea, some of it dribbling on to her chin. Gradually her circulation improved and she began to feel better. Voices murmured, 'Her colour's improved. . .' 'Another life saved, Doctor.' She smiled up at the bending faces.

'I think it would be a good idea if you gave Miss Grant some air.' David's voice was firm. Familiar faces moved away. 'You stay, Angie,' he ordered.

It was so lovely to lean against him and feel his arm about her that she wanted to stay like that forever, but when he saw her strength had returned he removed it. She wanted to cry 'Put it back, hold me close', and felt like weeping because she couldn't.

David misunderstood the misery in her eyes. 'It's all right.' His gentle voice brought the tears closer. 'I'm sure nine and a half lengths will count. Now try and stand.' His arm was about her again, helping her to her feet. She didn't need to lean against him but she did, just this one more time. 'Good girl,' he said. Then, looking at Angie, he said, 'When you've helped Holly to dress bring her to my car. Now, young lady.' He transferred his gaze to Holly. How she hated that expression. It was one of her father's, though he had not used it lately. Perhaps he had realised she had grown up. Perhaps David hadn't. 'Take your time. I'll wait for you in the car park.'

Holly did not demur; didn't say she would catch the bus; she was too weary.

'What a scare you gave us,' said Angie as they went into the changing-room.

'It was my own fault. I haven't had anything to eat since lunch.'

'Holly!' Angie was aghast. 'You should know better.'

It took a little longer than usual to dress as Holly found her fingers were clumsy. She was glad she had brought a thick sweater with her, though even with it on she felt cold.

David sprang out of the car as they approached. After settling Holly in the passenger-seat, he said, 'Can we give you a lift, Angie?'

'No, thanks,' Angie said shyly, 'I'm meeting Mike.'

'Ah.' He smiled. 'I hope you're encouraging him to study.'

'That's what we're going to do.' Angie sounded defensive.

He patted her shoulder. 'I'm sure you are.' And the sincerity in his voice took the stiffness from her face and she smiled.

Holly expected David to take the Sheeplaw turn-off but he passed it and went left into Market street, shortly afterwards drawing up outside a block of flats.

He replied to the question in her eyes. 'A little bird told me that you missed your tea.' He switched off the ignition. 'That accounts for your near-collapse.' He was not smiling.

It could have been Angie who'd told him, but she hadn't had time.

'The ward was too busy to leave and I would have held up the swim if I'd stopped to eat,' she said defensively. Then, looking out of the window, she asked, crossly, 'Why are we stopping here?'

'Because I don't want another fainted body on my hands,' he explained patiently. He pulled down the passenger-shade, which had a mirror on its back. 'Look at yourself.'

A pinched, pale face stared back at her from tired eyes. A slight smile touched her lips. 'I see what you mean.'

'I'll take you home when you've had a meal.' He climbed from the car and came round to open her door. 'I'm quite a good cook.'

Holly hesitated. 'You live here?' It certainly did not look like a retaurant.

'Yes.' His eyes were amused. 'We can't very well go to a restaurant with you looking like that, can we? You'd scare the customers away.'

He was right. But it was a nervous Holly who joined

him. As they approached the building he slipped his arm around her waist. At her startled glance he said, a mischievous twinkle in his eye, 'Just in case.'

'I don't think it's necessary now.' She put his arm firmly aside, not because she did not want it there, but because she wanted it there too much and didn't want him to suspect it.

The lift took them quickly and silently to the third floor. The doors opened soundlessly, and their feet left no prints on the thick carpet.

He unlocked the door of a flat and ushered her in. The hall carpet was brown. Muted shades of beige and cream coloured the walls and woodwork. Good prints of the moors hung on the walls.

The conventional décor of the hall did not prepare her for the lounge. A cream leather suite, black ash wall-unit, matching coffee-table, grey carpet, and curtains in a bold design incorporating colours of red, grey and black to tone with the décor. A beautifully sculptured white porcelain figure of a mother and child stood at the end of a white mantelpiece. She could just see a small dining area to the side.

It was a man's room. Definite in taste and ideas. Hard and tough, with just that touch of gentleness. There was a starkness that the scattered newspapers and medical journals did little to relieve.

He watched her expressive face. 'You don't like it, do you?' His eyes narrowed.

She could have prevaricated, have muttered an innocuous rejoiner, but her innate honesty would not let her. 'No. It's too modern for me.'

He laughed. 'The bathroom's second on the left off the hall, and the bedroom's opposite if you want a decent mirror.'

Did she look such a wreck? Perhaps it was a hint, and she found, as she looked in the bathroom mirror, that it was. She had not bothered much at the pool to amend her appearance.

So she sponged her face in his blue-tiled bathroom, and dried it on his fluffy blue towel; peeped into his cupboard over the sink and found he used the same toothpaste as she did. Then she could not resist going into the bedroom. He was right—the light was better in here.

Her eyes were drawn to the divan bed; it was big, long and wide. The black and grey theme was carried through in the striped duvet cover and curtains. Her pulse quickened as images rose in her mind—caressing images, which she hurriedly suppressed.

Averting her head, she caught sight of her flushed face in a mirror on top of a black ash chest of drawers. Her feet sank into the pale grey carpet as she moved closer. Silver brushes lay like pools of light on the dark top; a hairpin, the sort used to hold long hair in place, was caught under one of them. A small gasp escaped her lips. There was only one woman Holly knew who used such pins; Christine Nicol. So the rumours were true. David was the ward sister's lover.

Holly sighed. A sadness swept over her and drained the recently renewed colour from her cheeks. What a way to discover you are in love, she thought.

She could not refute the evidence before her eyes. The whole hospital knew. She had even seen it for herself, the way Christine had looked at David, his solicitousness towards her. And hadn't they been in London together?

She reached into her bag for her brush and applied it vigorously, bringing tears to her eyes, or were they tears of lost hope? She put the brush down. I must compose myself. So David was another's. So she would have to suppress her longings and really grow up.

Straightening her clothes and holding her head high, she went to find the consultant.

He was in the kitchen. Pine units glowed softly, fresh green curtains hung at the window. Her face lit with pleasure.

'This more to your taste?' he asked. He wore a green and white striped apron and was beating eggs.

'Definitely.'

A small pine table fitted companionably in front of the corner seat. An uncorked bottle of wine, a basket of sliced French bread and a prepared salad were set out on the table.

'Is there anything I can do to help?' she asked.

'You can put out the knives and forks if you like.' He gestured towards a drawer.

'You'll make someone a well-trained husband one of these days,' she quipped, and wished she had not tried to be clever when he replied,

'Oh, I intend to.' The whisk sounded as brisk as his voice. Christine, no doubt, Holly thought, turning to the cupboard in case he saw the pain she was sure must be showing in her eyes.

The hiss and spit of the whisked eggs hitting the pan sounded like hostile mockery.

Holly set the table. David poured a glass of wine and pushed it towards her. 'This'll put the colour back into your cheeks,' he said, smiling.

It isn't wine I need, she thought but lifted the glass. He raised his to her and they drank. The heat from the frying-pan had brought a light sheen of perspiration to his brow.

'Madam,' he said, placing his glass on the table and bowing, 'take your seat.'

She smiled and obeyed him. He took a fluffy omelette out of the pan and presented it to her with a flourish. 'Don't wait for me,' he said. 'Mine won't take a minute.'

Holly had only taken a couple of mouthfuls when he joined her. 'This is delicious,' she complimented him.

He grinned, his fork halfway to his mouth. 'Don't look so surprised. Most of the best chefs are men.'

If only she could be as relaxed as he was. His nearness was disturbing her greatly. His vitality was almost palpable. To distract herself she said, 'Mike mentioned that you lived in London for a time.' She took a sip of wine.

'Yes.' He swallowed a mouthful. 'Our parents were doctors. They came from Yorkshire.'

'Oh.' She was surprised. 'You haven't got a Yorkshire accent, though.' He made to refill her glass but she covered it with her hand.

'Doctor's orders.' She removed her hand and the wine flowed. 'Blame the public school for that.' He set the bottle back on the table, his eyes studying her face. 'You wouldn't know you were a Yorkshire lass either,' he said.

'Same reason.' She smiled slightly. She needed to say something to relieve the tension that was creeping between them, so continued, 'You mentioned buying a house, so are you planning on staying here now?' She placed her knife and fork together.

'Yes.'

He didn't enlarge upon this and she felt rebuffed into saying defensively, 'I wasn't prying, just trying to get to know you.'

He leaned towards her. 'Oh? Why?'

'It makes for good ward relations if you know your consultant,' she improvised quickly.

'I'm disappointed,' he said. 'I thought it was the man you wanted to know.'

Holly couldn't decide if he was serious; something in

the tone of his voice, an inflextion perhaps, made her think he was, but his eyes were laughing. He must be teasing. She felt she was floundering for a second time this evening, and this time she was more than out of her depth.

He reached across the table and took her hand. 'Don't look so worried. I was only teasing.'

So she had been right.

He rose and collected the plates. 'What about some cheese in the lounge?' he suggested. 'Take your wine.'

'I'd rather coffee, please.'

'Afraid I might take advantage of your inebriation?'

She knew he was teasing this time, so decided to join in the game. She had risen to carry the salad bowl to the sink and was standing beside him.

'Yes,' she said, smiling cheekily up at him. 'That you'll. . . Her voice assumed the tone associated with romantic films, and, placing a hand over her heart, she said, 'That you'll take me in your arms and kiss the breath out of me.' She was laughing now.

'Oh?' He was smiling. 'Like this?'

His arms were around her before she could do more than look astonished. His lips were upon hers before she could gasp. It wasn't a gentle kiss, either. It was demanding, and as her blood pounded in her veins her skin became alive with sensations, fear touched her— not of him, but of herself. She was powerless, soft, malleable in his hands. She melted into him, wanted him, longed for him. When he released her she was bemused, dazed and breathless.

'How does that compare with Andrew?' he said drily.

The only kiss Andrew had given her had been gentle, unsure. David's question took her by surprise and she replied without thinking and as a way of protection, 'Quite well, really,' and blushed.

David didn't answer, but there was an amused expression in his eyes that told her he didn't believe her, and she was annoyed. When he did speak it was to say he would make the coffee. 'Take this into the lounge, will you?' He handed her the cheese-board. 'And put a match to the fire.'

In the lounge, she drew the curtains, shutting out the twinkling town lights. It had started to rain and the drops on the window-pane looked like silent tears and depressed her. The gas flame cheered her up and gave warmth to the stark room, as did the pearl-coloured wall lights. The black furniture became less severe.

Suddenly she longed to be back in her own home, in her own lounge with its comfortable familiarity. This room threatened somehow.

Holly didn't hear David come in, the carpet was so thick. It was the clatter of the the tray as he set it on the coffee-table that started her, and she jumped.

'I don't usually have that effect on young women.' There was a hint of mockery in his voice.

Holly forced a smile. 'You shouldn't have such thick carpets.' She crossed to the couch and sat down.

He took the seat beside her and examined her face. 'You look very tired; are you all right?'

His concern brought tears close to the surface and she said, 'I'm fine. A cup of coffee, a little cheese and I'll be ready for home.' She tried to sound chirpy and smiled, but it was a tremulous smile.

He did not put his arm around her and she was glad. She could not have borne that. He passed a full cup to her and pushed the cheese-board closer. It was difficult to swallow the cloying Cheddar, but she managed it, and drank her coffee.

Holly felt better when they left the flat. It had stopped raining and the air was fresh. She breathed deeply.

David hardly spoke on the way to Sheeplaw and she was grateful. It was hard enough trying to look cheerful without having to sound it.

'Thanks for everything,' she said as he stopped outside her home.

'Think nothing of it,' he said lightly. 'I make a habit of rescuing drowning maidens.' The street lights were near enough for her to see his smile.

'I hope you're there if it happens again,' she quipped.

'You'd better invite me when you next plan to swim, then.' He grinned and winked.

She expected him to drive away when she stepped from the car, but he joined her and took the key from her hand.

'Can't have anyone running off with you. The hospital's short of nurses.'

She smiled. His blue eyes became serious, and, taking her by the shoulders, he kissed her forehead.

'My father does that,' she said spontaneously.

'We older people do seem to follow a pattern.' He smiled again. 'Goodnight, Holly.' His tone was so gentle that she hardly heard him.

She waited on the step until his car's tail-lights disappeared.

The sponsored events were a great success. The money raised, though not quite enough, was an admirable sum. A local businessman donated the rest; his wife had been a patient in Harrington General.

Holly missed the ceremony when the cheque was handed over because she was on night duty. During the next week all she saw of David was a quick glimpse and a waved hand.

As she crept round the ward with her torch in the silence broken only by an occasional whispered,

'Nurse,' she tried to convince herself that it was not love she felt for David but sexual attraction.

Christine was on a week's holiday. Holly had taken the report from Janet Roberts, who was staffing in Holly's place. Nurse Bailey, who was on nights with Holly, had left to prepare the night drinks.

'Have you heard the latest?' Janet's eyes gleamed.

Holly had not slept too well that day; builders were working near by. 'What about?' she asked snappily.

'Sister Nicol and David Quinn.'

That shook the weariness from Holly. 'Oh?'

Encouraged, Janet continued, 'They've been seen together.' Her eyes were round with anticipation.

'Oh, is that all?' Holly's tone was dismissive.

'Coming out of a London hotel together.'

'So?' Holly picked up the temperature book, feigning uninterest, though the opposite was how she felt.

'Don't you mind?' Janet was gazing at her with astonishment.

'Mind? Why should I?' Holly frowned.

'Well. . . I thought. . .' Janet paused uncertainly. 'The word had it that you and David Quinn were. . .' She didn't continue—Holly's face stopped her.

'Well, of all the. . .' Holly was glad of the anger which burst from her; it relieved the pain. She slapped the TPR book down on the desk. 'That just goes to show how false rumours can be. I'm not interested in David Quinn.' She emphasised each word. 'We were just thrown together to organise the sponsored events; nothing more. Would you mind. . .?' She indicated that she wanted to sit at the desk.

Janet jumped up, blushing.

Holly took her seat and drew the Kardex towards her. Glancing up at Janet, she said, 'Do me a favour and squash that rumour. I'm going out with Andrew

McLean and it wouldn't be fair to him if he heard that bit of hospital gossip.'

'Oooh!' Janet's face brightened. 'I'll do my best.'

After the staff nurse had gone and Holly was making a work list, she wished she had not mentioned Andrew. She was seeing him occasionally, but that was all. There wasn't anything serious between them, not as Holly's tone had implied. She frowned. Well, on her side there wasn't. She tapped her chin with the biro, thinking about the last time she had seen him. He had taken her to the cinema, and the arm he had placed around her shoulders had had a possessive feel about it. Sighing, she pushed the male sex from her mind and concentrated on her work.

At two in the morning the theatre phoned to say they were sending a patient down. 'It's a repair of an abdominal stab wound. He's on full blood at the moment. Mr Quinn thinks he's stable enough to move. His name's Donaldson.'

'Thanks,' said Holly, replacing the receiver.

It wasn't long before she heard trolley wheels coming down the corridor; they made a squeak that would not have been heard during the daytime activity.

She darted out of the ward, where she had been helping Jean prepare the bed, and met it as it reached the office. David, still in Theatre greens, was holding the blood steady. Holly recognised the theatre staff nurse; they'd trained together.

The patient was transferred to the bed as quietly as possible. Their shadows moved as the small light at the top of the bed threw its beam. The curtains swayed as they touched them.

'Thanks, Henry.' David smiled at the male nurse, who was manoeuvring the trolley out of the ward.

Holly's surprise at seeing David when she'd thought he was on holiday was put aside as she took the patient's blood-pressure and pulse. He was so young—seventeen according to his notes. What had happened? Well built, with a sensitive face, he did not appear the sort of youth to be mixed up in a knife fight.

Holly raised troubled eyes to David's. He answered her unspoken question. 'Apparently he was attacked for no reason.' The compassion she felt was mirrored in his eyes. A smile of recognition passed between them. At least we have a professional bond, she thought. I'll just have to make do with that. 'I'll be in the office,' he said.

She nodded. She knew he would wait until he was sure his patient was safe. Jimmy's eyes watched her as she checked the blood transfusion. She smiled down at him.

'Why?' he whispered, his eyes perplexed.

He looked like a child, lying there with the sheet up to his chin, his dark hair damp, clinging to this head. She stroked a stray strand back from his forehead and said softly, 'I don't know, Jimmy. Perhaps the police do.' She smiled down at him gently. 'Try not to worry. You'll be quite safe here.'

The confidence in her face and voice reassured him and he closed his eyes. Nurse Bailey was hovering near by.

'Stay with Jimmy, will you, please?' Holly instructed, amnd was pleased to see how calm her junior was this time; Jean's confidence was growing.

As Holly made her way to the office she frowned; something was niggling at her and it was not the thought of David waiting for her. He was sprawled in the armchair, his eyes closed. That's how he must look when he is asleep, she thought. I wonder what it would be like to wake up beside him? He opened his eyes and smiled. She blushed. She longed to kneel at his feet, kiss the tired lines away, but, even as she returned his smile, the spectre of Christine Nicol stood between them, here in this office, which was so particularly her own. Her plant was on the window-sill, her calendar was on the wall, her pens and pencils in the desk-tidy. How could Holly compete with such a sophisticated presence, a woman accomplished in her profession, and more David's age?

'Staff!' Nurse Bailey's voice came from the door.

Holly swung towards her, immediately alert to the anxious tone of her junior's voice. David sprang to his feet.

'It's Mr Donaldson—Jimmy.' Jean's face was white. 'Blood. . .'

David and Holly did not wait to hear more; they rushed into the ward.

The patient's eyes were closed, his dark lashes black against the pallor of his cheeks, his skin cold, clammy. Rapidly David took Jimmy's blood-pressure; it had dropped, his pulse had risen to a hundred and twenty, thin and thready. David tore back the bedclothes and whipped off the soaked dressing. The wound was intact but bright red blood was welling from a tiny puncture wound in a crease at the side of his abdomen.

David replaced the dressing. 'Pads.' His voice was urgent as he hauled the foot of the bed up and pushed a chair under it.

Holly must have known this was going to happen for she had put a pile of sterile pads on the bed-side table. There was no time to wash her hands. She ripped the packets open and thrust the pads towards him.

'Phone Theatre. Tell them the patient's haemorrhaging and that we're bringing him straight up in the bed,' David instructed, layering the pads.

Holly nodded to Jean, who sped away.

'I knew something was wrong,' David was muttering. 'How could I have missed it?' He sounded defeated.

'It was so small that it had probably congealed. The blood transfusion must have opened it,' she whispered.

He lifted the bed down with a grunt, his face grim. They rushed the bed to Theatre, where Henry took over. David was stripping off his gown as Holly left.

Back in the office, she sank down on the chair. Had Jimmy's collapse been her fault? Had she missed something? No, she thought. The patient's condition had been stable when she had left Nurse Bailey with him. Then doubts crept into her mind again. Had those few minutes taken gazing at David's face distracted her? Had she allowed her emotions to affect her judgement?

'Staff!' Jean Bailey was trying to hide her anxiety. 'Will he be all right?' A tear threatened. 'I feel so guilty. Perhaps I should have done more.'

Her putting into words Holly's musings gave the staff nurse confidence. She jumped up and placed an arm round her junior. 'You did splendidly,' she enthused, pushing Jean into the vacated chair. 'If you hadn't acted so quickly Jimmy would be dead.' The certainty in her voice convinced the young nurse, whose face brightened. 'And I shall say so in my report.'

'Thanks, Staff.' Jean's smile was tremulous.

'I'll just do a quick ward round, then make you a cup of tea.'

Jean leapt to her feet. 'Oh, I couldn't let you do that,' she said. 'I'll make the tea.'

Holly thought it best to let her, and went into the ward. Surprisingly it was quiet. Thank goodness it wasn't post-op night. As Holly reached Mr Martin's bed—he was to have a partial gastrectomy next day—he whispered, 'Did that patient. . .' he nodded towards the space where the bed had been '. . .have the operation I'm having?' His eyes were very anxious.

'No, Mr Martin,' she reassured him as she turned his

pillow and straightened his crumpled sheets. The nursing staff did not discuss other patients' cases, but Holly thought more harm would be done if she did not allay Mr Martin's anxiety, so she said, 'The young man had a stab wound.'

Relief eased the anxious lines from the middle-aged face looking up at her. 'Thanks for telling me, Staff.'

Holly wished him goodnight and carried on towards the kitchen. Nurse Bailey had just made the tea. They discussed the early-morning routine work while they drank it in the office.

Jean went off to the label the urine jars used to collect specimens from those patients going to Theatre. Holly was charting the temperatures when she heard the trolley. It could not be her patient back, surely? He would have gone to Intensive Care. She opened the office door and met David, pushing the empty bed.

'I volunteered to return this,' he said, smiling. 'The theatre staff were tired.'

He looked more than tired himself. One of the things she liked about David was that he wasn't officious, didn't patronise, and would help out where he could. After assisting her to position the bed he followed her back to the office. 'Thought you'd like to know that we saved him.' It was said with quiet simplicity.

'I'm so glad.'

'You're a good nurse, Holly Grant,' he said, smiling. His words pleased her, but she had to say, 'Nurse Bailey's the heroine tonight.'

He nodded his agreement, but said, 'One of these days you'll be an excellent ward sister if some vet doesn't snap you up and marry you.'

'That's highly unlikely.' Her tone was abupt. Marriage to anyone other than the man standing opposite her was unthinkable.

'Oh?' It was a question. 'Love-life not going too smoothly?'

Was he interested or just curious? 'Probably as smoothly as yours,' she answered sweetly.

He placed a hand on his heart. 'But I have no love-life without you,' he said, his eyes full of mischief, copying her dramatic pose in the flat. She blushed as she remembered what had followed.

She laughed to cover the confusion and only wished his words were true; some of this wishing must have shown in her eyes, for his face became serious. He had discarded his Theatre greens and was wearing a navy blue polo-necked sweater of fine wool that clung to his athletic chest, and his grey trousers emphasised the slimness of his hips.

He moved towards her and she knew he was going to take her in his arms. She didn't want that, for he would discover how she felt about him—she wouldn't have been able to conceal it. So she turned from him, lifted her torch, and said, 'I must do the ward round.'

He caught her arm as she made for the door. 'Must you?' His voice was urgent.

She sensed he was still tense from dealing with the emergency, when hand, brain and eye had had to be co-ordinated like a finely tuned machine. But he wasn't a machine, and she could feel his need.

'Night Sister's round is due.' Her voice was but a whisper.

The insistence of his expression silenced her. She wanted him to kiss her so very much; wanted to feel his arms around her. She too had her needs. He was close enough for her to see herself mirrored in his eyes, and could feel the blood pounding in her throat with anticipation. A crash from the ward. Alarm wiped desire from their faces. She was out of the office with

David behind her and into the ward. Restless movements, moans and a muttered, 'Can't you keep quiet?' came from the darkened beds.

Nurse Bailey crept from behind the screened patient. 'I'm terribly sorry, Staff.' Her pale face was stricken. 'I'm afraid I dropped a bedpan.'

'I trust it was empty,' said David laconically.

Holly had trouble containing her laughter.

'Oh, yes,' whispered Jean, her expression earnest.

'What about a cup of tea?' came from the gloom as more heads popped up.

'I'd better go,' said David, smiling. 'You've got your hands full here.'

'Yes,' replied Holly, laughter in her voice.

After the ward doors had closed gently behind him, Holly went from patient to patient, quietening them, shaking a pillow here, giving a drink there. She was grateful for Jean Bailey's clumsiness. A kiss, at a moment of high tension, was not what she wanted from David Quinn. She wanted more.

CHAPTER SEVEN

HOLLY decided to push thoughts of David Quinn out of her mind, and being on night duty helped. On her nights off she went out with her father or Andrew, but felt a bit guilty about the young vet, knowing she was using him to distract herself from thinking about David.

The demonstration against closure of the veterinary school fell on some of her nights off. She was standing beside Andrew, holding a placard which read 'SAVE OUR VET SCHOOL' in large red letters, one cold Saturday morning. Andrew put his arm about her.

'We do have fun, don't we, Holly?' he said.

Even as she answered, 'Yes,' her conscience smote her.

The other students jostled them, throwing her against him; his arm tightened. She must say something now, to show him that she only looked upon him as a friend.

'We do have a good time,' she smiled into the eyes level with her own, 'and I value your friendship, but I hope I haven't led you to think there was more to it than that.'

Jack Thomas, the organiser of the demonstration, pushed between them, preventing Andrew from answering, but Holly saw what looked like consternation on the young vet's face.

'Come on,' Jack shouted above the noise of the Saturday traffic, grabbing Holly's arm. 'We can't keep a beauty like you at the back. We need to draw the crowd.' His university scarf blew across her face, the fringe touching her eye; immediately it watered and blurred.

'Oh, I'm sorry, Holly.' Jack was contrite.

Before she could console him a hand took hold of her arm, and she thought it was his until David's voice said, 'Let me have a look at it.'

'Hey, wait a minute!' Jack's voice was shrill.

'It's all right,' said Holly, both eyes now streaming. 'It's Mr Quinn. He's the consultant on my ward.'

Her banner was taken from her and must have been thrust at Jack, for she heard David say, 'Take that,' in a rough voice before she was led away.

'Stand still while I open the car door,' David said.

She heard the click of the lock, and then he was pushing her gently into the car. A scent, faint but familiar, wafted towards her; she recognised the perfume; it was Christine's.

'It looks awfully sore.' Christine's voice, full of concern, came from beside her, and Holly felt a tissue pressed into her hand.

'Thanks,' she muttered, mopping her face.

'Don't rub it,' Christine advised.

The engine started. 'We'll take you to Casualty and have a look at it in case there's a scratch on the cornea.' His deep voice came from the front.

'It was lucky we were passing and saw the incident,' said Christine.

Holly felt intrusive and uncomfortable. 'I don't want to put you out,' she said, frowning with pain. 'I'm sure Andrew could take me to the hospital.' She patted her eyes. 'We were parted in the crush but he'll be along in a minute.' The tissue was wringing wet.

'We couldn't possibly desert a member of the ward staff, could we, Christine?' David said in a teasing way.

'No, indeed,' Christine replied. 'Anyway, we were only going house-hunting and they'll still be there when we've attended to you.' Christine's voice was even, but Holly thought she detected an underlying stiffness.

So marriage must be in their minds, decided Holly, and the thought added to the misery of her painful eye. She was glad when the car stopped. David assisted her out and the three of them went into Accident and Emergency.

'Can I help, sir?'

Holly recognised the casualty sister's voice; it held a note of curiosity.

'No, thanks, Sister,' said David. 'You're busy enough.' Nurse Grant has hurt her eye. Sister Nicol can help me if it should be necessary.'

Holly knew they were in one of the cubicles when he said, 'The bed's behind you, Holly,' and felt his hand assist her up. 'I'll use a floret.'

She heard him wash his hands, heard the packet opened, and saw, through her haze, his fingers holding the small stick coming nearer and nearer. She felt her eyelid lifted, and raised her hands, not to ward him off, but more as a reflex action. They were trembling.

'It's all right, Holly.' David's voice was very gentle. 'I'll not hurt you.'

She felt the stick touch her eye and knew the fluorescence would show up any scratches. After a moment to allow it to work David lifted the lid again and examined her eye with the opthalmoscope.

'You'll be relieved to hear that there isn't a mark to be seen.'

'Good,' she whispered, but it was very sore and the lid was swollen. 'Thank you.'

'I'll go for some eye ointment. Sister will stay with you.'

Holly heard the swish of the curtains as he left. Her other eye was watering in sympathy and her cheeks were wet.

'I'm just going to dab your face,' Christine warned.

'Thanks,' Holly murmured. Her head was beginning to ache.

She recognised David's footsteps returning and a small draught of air touched her face as he parted the curtains.

'I'm just going to squeeze some Chloromycetin ointment along the lid,' he said. He applied it so carefully that she hardly felt it. He was very gentle for such a big man.

'We'll take you home now,' Christine said.

She even *sounds* like his wife, Holly thought as she pushed herself into a sitting position. 'I'm sure I can manage on my own if I just wait a bit for it to settle,' she said.

The curtains swung aside and Andrew's voice, full of concern, came closer, 'Jack told me Mike's brother brought you here. Are you all right?'

He was just a blur to her. 'I'm fine,' she said, slipping her legs over the side of the bed. 'Ready to go home.' She sounded as if she was delighted he'd come, which she was. Now she could escape from David. The harmony between him and Christine was disturbing. There seemed to be a bond between them.

She looked in the direction she supposed David and Christine to be in and said, 'Thank you very much for helping me,' in a formal voice.

'I believe this is the second time Mr Quinn has rescued you, Staff,' said Christine. There was a sharpness in her tone.

So David had told her, mused Holly. I wonder if he also mentioned the kiss. Probably not; after all, it had not been sincere, had it?

Andrew put his arm about her. She leant against him, grateful for his warm sympathy. 'Andrew will take me home,' she said.

They made a handsome couple—young, alert, well matched—or so David thought. Holly did not see the bleakness that touched the consultant's eyes, and if she had been able to she would not have associated it with herself. She knew he found her attractive, even desirable, but she did not know how he really felt, how her brightness, intelligence and courage had affected him. She made him feel years younger, like the man he had been the year his parents' death had robbed him of his youth. He could reclaim it with her, but had he the right? He was twelve years her senior, and then there was his commitment to Christine. He felt her hand on his arm now.

'We can go, then, David. I'm sure Holly's boyfriend will look after her.'

David straightened his shoulders. 'Yes.' He held out the eye ointment to Andrew. 'See she applies this four-hourly.'

Holly's sight was clearing. She intercepted the tiny tube, her fingers touching David's; they felt cold. She looked up at him quickly, but the sudden movement made both her eyes water and she couldn't see his expression.

'I can manage,' she said firmly. 'Dad can help me.'

As her sight improved again she saw Christine standing with her arm through David's. They looked complete, and when he patted her hand the gesture appeared intimate. Holly's misery deepened.

They all left together, the younger couple in front. Holly could hear Christine's heels tap-tapping behind her, and quickened her own pace, eager to be away from them, and only wished she could banished the picture of David looking affectionately down at Christine from her mind as easily.

Andrew was very attentive on the drive home. 'Are you all right? Would you like to stop for a cup of tea?'

'No, thank you, Andrew,' she said, controlling her voice because she felt like screaming—his sedate driving was aggravating her.

He was driving his father's car, a family saloon, and Holly could visualise his having one similar in a few years' time. There was no dash, no verve about him, but he would make a good husband. Perhaps she should encourage him, but she knew she wouldn't.

When they arrived at her home he said, 'Let me come in and make you a cup of tea. Let me look after you, Holly.' There was a pleading in the way that he said it that worried her.

'No, thanks, Andrew. Dad's in.' Impulsively she went to kiss his cheek, but he moved his head so that their lips met instead, disconcerting her.

'You didn't mean what you said, Holly, did you?' he asked.

His face was so vulnerable that she wanted to say no, but answered firmly, 'I'm afraid I did,' and felt the pain she saw in his eyes.

'We can still be friends, though, can't we?'

She didn't like the eagerness she heard in his voice but couldn't deny him that, so said, 'Yes.'

As she waved his car away she thought how different his kiss had been from David's, whose had stirred her very being.

By the time her nights off had finished her eye was better. She took the report from Christine and wondered if she had found a house. She could not resist asking, 'I hope I didn't delay you too much on Saturday,' as she was taking the keys from Christine.

'Not at all.' The ward sister was looking more relaxed, not as pale as usual. 'We saw quite a few houses.'

Holly looked interested, hoping Christine would tell her more, but she didn't; she had risen and seemed in a hurry to be away. There was a knock, followed by the door's opening; David stood there. Holly's heartbeat quickened.

He was a study in black and grey, with his dark hair, grey suit, black shirt and grey tie. He was incredibly handsome, but it was more than that; there was a depth to him. How straight he stands, Holly thought; how blue his eyes are.

He was looking at Christine. 'Ready?' he asked, smiling.

Christine picked up her pen and put it in her pocket. 'For you—always,' she said, and Holly heard the truth underlying the teasing note.

After they had left Holly found it difficult to concentrate. Christine was in love with David. The realisation shook her. Thank goodness I'm on holiday as soon as I come off night duty, she thought, and brightened. The relationship between her father and herself had grown in warmth and understanding. They were going to Cyprus together. She hoped that on her return she would be able to view David with equanimity, but would she ever be able to do that? Sighing, she went about her duties.

The holiday was a great success. They discovered how companionable they were. Both liked exploring, enjoyed a sense of history, laughed at the same things. Holly returned in good spirits and was looking forward to being on day duty.

Holly was on the late shift a few days later. The evenings were drawing in and there was a chill in the air. Holly shivered as she came out of the office as the last visitor was leaving. She was just about to enter the ward when the phone rang. Nurse Bailey was hurrying to answer it, but Holly said through the open door, 'I'll get it.'

Afterwards she wondered if the shiver she had felt had been a premonition.

'Holly?' It was Johnny Simpson. He was casualty officer and had joked with her that morning, threatening to keep her busy.

'Yes, Johnny?' She was laughing. 'I hope you're not carrying out your promise.'

'Holly.' There was no answering laughter in his voice and her heart missed a beat. 'Sit down, Holly.'

She sank into the chair; its feet scraped a little; her hand holding the receiver tightened. No one knew how she felt about David so it must be her father.

'Dad?' Her breath hissed between her teeth as she drew it in.

There was a pause while Johnny braced himself. 'A drunk driver swerved across the road into your father's oncoming car.' He sighed. 'Your father has a severe head injury. David's examining him now. He thinks there's a sub-arachnoid haemorrhage there and, if it's confirmed by X-ray, he'll operate.'

'But wouldn't a neurosurgeon be——'

Johnny interrupted her. 'David *is* a neurosurgeon—didn't you know? He's a damn good one, too.'

She didn't answer; her mind was numb.

'I don't know how to tell you this, Holly, but the driver of the other car is to be admitted to your ward. He is concussed and has a broken arm. He's to have the usual observations taken. I'm so sorry, but you have the only empty bed.'

Holly swallowed. 'Oh.' Did this strange-sounding voice belong to her? She was cold, and the numbness was spreading, threatening to engulf her. She felt as if she were outside herself, looking down at this staff nurse.

'Your father's to go to Intensive Care following the operation. Hold on a minute. . .' She could hear muttered words but could not distinguish what was said.

'Holly, this is David.' Her name was spoken gently, yet, at the same time, with firmness. She had heard that tone before; he had used it when he had had to break bad news to a relative before.

'No. . .no.' There was a sob in her voice. 'He's not dead.'

'No.' The gentleness had gone from his voice, but the firmness was still there. 'I'm not going to deceive you; his chances are slim.'

'Oh. . .' It was a heart-breaking sound.

'I've phoned the SNO. She's sending you a relief.'

'I must see my father, but afterwards I'd like to come back to the ward. You'll be in Theatre for some time, and I'd rather have something to do.'

He didn't argue. He just said, 'All right. One of the nurses from here will relieve you for now. You'll have to come and sign your father's consent form. I'll let the SNO know of your decision.'

'Thanks,' she whispered.

Holly was replacing the receiver when Nurse Bailey came in with the urine-testing book.

'Are you all right?' she exclaimed. 'You're as white as a sheet.'

'My father's had an accident; a car went into his.' Her voice sounded incredulous. Things like this didn't happen to nurses, just to the general public. She knew it was ridiculous to think like that, but couldn't help it; it just flashed into her mind. She had seen the results of crashes caused by drunk drivers—the pathetic broken bodies—when she had worked in Casualty. But that her father should be a victim she found hard to believe.

Black spots appeared before her eyes. She heard Jean's voice say from a distance, 'I'm terribly sorry.'

Felt the junior put an arm round her shoulders. 'I'll make you a cup of tea.' Heard her leave, and still couldn't believe her father was lying in Casualty.

Holly fought against the faintness, and had succeeded in righting the room by the time Jean returned with a steaming mug. She had drunk half of it and was feeling better when she heard the trolley. The admission had slipped her mind.

Angie's head came round the door. 'Holly, I'm so sorry.'

Everyone used the same words when tragedy struck, thought Holly. I'd never realised that before.

Angie came forward with the notes, her eyes compassionate. 'I'm even more sorry to bring you this patient.' She paused. Her friend's white face worried her. 'The SNO wants me to take over from you,' she said.

Holly rose and held out her hand for the notes. It was as if she had not heard what Angie was saying.

'Is this the man?'

Angie nodded.

Holly flicked the folder open. George Brady, aged forty-six. Did he have a daughter? Was he a father?

'I'll go and see him.' She took a step forward.

Angie barred her way. 'D'you think you should?'

She looked at her friend, and Angie, seeing how near to breaking-point Holly was, stepped back, shocked by her friend's stricken face.

'I have to see him,' Holly said, feeling she had to explain.

Mr Brady had been placed in the emergency bed. Jean was attempting to wrap the sphygmomanometer cuff around his upper arm, but the patient was flinging it about and hitting out.

'Don't do that,' he said crossly in a slurred voice.

What was she doing here? Holly thought. This man's

responsible for my father's severe injuries. She stood immobile, watching Angie go to the side of the bed, heard her say, 'Mr Brady,' in a firm voice, heard his belligerent reply, 'What d'you want?'

The professional part of Holly's mind registered cerebral irritation due to his concussion, but the shocked person who inhabited her body did nothing to help the struggling nurses. Suddenly Mr Brady reared on to his side and was sick on the floor, his broken arm in its temporary plaster hitting the bed.

'Aaaaah!' he yelled in pain.

The smell of beer-laden vomit, acrid and stale, filled the air.

'Fetch a bowl quickly, Nurse,' Angie ordered as she pulled the patient back from the edge of the bed, clicking the cot-sides into place.

Holly could do nothing to help. It was as if she were turned to stone. All the action before her seemed to be happening in slow motion. Angie's tightening of the cuff, recording the blood-pressure. Angie's checking that his pupils were reacting to light using her pencil torch, with some difficulty, as he was moving his head from side to side.

Jean returned with the bowl. 'I'll fetch the mop, shall I?' she said, handing it to Angie, who nodded.

The vomiting seemed to have settled Mr Brady, for he had closed his eyes. He doesn't look like a potential killer, with his brown hair streaked with grey and his round face turning flabby, thought Holly.

Her arm was pulled and she frowned in irritation. She was trying to concentrate. There was something she had to do.

'Come on, Holly.' It was Angie's hand on her arm. 'You must go to Casualty.'

Ah, that was it. Holly's mind cleared. The numbness

left her and she was filled with pain. She looked so pathetic that Angie's eyes filled with tears in sympathy.

'Jean can go with you,' she said, looking for the junior, who was just coming through the door, bucket and mop in hand.

Holly took a deep breath. 'No. I'll be all right now.'

She tried to make her feet move quickly, but they seemed to be encased in leaden shoes. When she reached Casualty, David came quickly towards her.

'Where have you been?' His voice was sharp with anxiety, but when he saw her pale, pinched face, dull eyes and lifeless hair he put his arm round her shoulder and led her to the cubicle. It was the one David had treated her eye in. Before he pulled the curtains aside he said, 'Prepare yourself, Holly.' He didn't explain. He didn't need to.

Every nerve in her body tensed as she approached the bed. She hardly recognised her father; a livid bruise discoloured one side of his face, which was grotesquely swollen. Unconscious, it was devoid of expression. He didn't look like her father and a wild hope rose within her. Perhaps there had been a mistake. Then she saw the ring. It was as familiar to her as her own face, and a forgotten childhood memory of sitting on his knee and twisting it round his finger rose unbidden in her mind.

A sob escaped her. David put his arm round her shoulder and held her tightly; a smell compounded of antiseptic and disinfectant clung to his coat; his stethoscope dug into her side.

'Sit down,' he commanded.

'No, I must go back to the ward.' Only there would she be safe. . .out of this nightmare. She tried to pull away, looking up at him as if he were a stranger, her eyes wild, anguished.

'Holly!' He drew her away from the bed, his voice

very firm. 'Pull yourself together, girl.' He took hold of her shoulders and shook her. 'Your father's going to need you if he survives.' The brutality of his words acted like cold water, clarifying her mind, and the awful enormity of the truth of what he had said brought the tears; her eyes glistened with them. Her silent grief was more terrible than her hysteria, and David's eyes smarted in sympathy. He wrapped her in his arms and whispered, 'I would give anything to spare you this.'

How comforting it was to rest against him, to draw strength from his compassion. It soothed away the shock. She lifted her head and tried to smile.

'That's my girl,' he said, his voice husky. He kissed her gently, tasting the salt of her tears.

Holly had never felt so lost. Normally she could cope with anything, but the strength she had inherited from the man lying immobile on the bed seemed to be draining away even as his was. She realised now how much she had relied upon him. Even when they were estranged he had been there like a rock. She had always known she could depend upon him.

As she rested in the security of David's arms an unbearable longing for him to take over, not as a father figure, but as a husband—a lover—took hold of her.

When he released her the coldness she felt was not only grief for her father, but for herself. She was losing both the men she loved, one possibly by death, the other by marriage to another. With an effort she looked up into David's face and whispered, 'Thank you.'

He touched her face with his hand and she longed to catch it, kiss it, but let him remove it without doing either.

Holly stayed with her father until he went to Theatre. All the while she sat beside him she thought of the wasted years and wished them back again, admitting that her grief was all the deeper because of the remorse she felt. She watched the nurses wheel the bed away, and was glad David was operating.

Holly didn't want to go back to the ward, but knew she must. The knowledge that she had broken her nurse's code was adding to her misery. She should have put aside her personal horror, should have helped Angie with Mr Brady.

Holly met her friend at the office door and saw the night staff sitting at the desk.

'All done.' Angie smiled as she linked her arm in Holly's.

'That man. . .?' It was an effort to talk or even think, but she must know.

Angie knew to whom she was referring. 'Mr Brady's stable,' she said, moving her arm to put it round Holly's shoulders. 'Come with me. I'll make you a drink. We'll let the theatre know we're at the nurses' home.'

Holly nodded, too tired to speak. After Angie had delivered her message the girls made their way to Angie's room. Holly sat down on the bed and looked so forlorn that her friend put down the kettle she was about to fill and sat beside her.

'Try not to worry,' she said. It was difficult for Angie to keep the distress from her voice. 'David will do his best.'

'I know.' Holly rested her head on Angie's shoulder, filled with a desperate weariness. She couldn't tell her friend about the remorse. . .the guilt she was feeling.

'A cup of tea is what you need,' said Angie brightly.

The sound of the water running into the kettle and then, when it had boiled, into the pot seemed to be magnified to Holly's ears. She hardly noticed Angie putting a full mug on the bedside cabinet.

'It's a bit hot,' Angie warned.

Holly wrapped her hands around the mug, hoping it

would warm them, and took a sip. It helped. She hadn't realised how dry her mouth had become.

Angie refilled it and sat beside her friend, but still Holly couldn't unburden herself. They didn't speak, but gradually Angie's silent sympathy relaxed Holly and she felt better.

A knock at the door, followed by, 'Phone for you, Angie,' brought them both to their feet.

'I'll take it,' Angie said, seeing the fear in her friend's eyes.

'No,' Holly insisted, and moved to the door.

It was a wall phone. The receiver was dangling, swinging to and fro, to and fro. Holly caught it up nad said, 'Nurse Grant speaking,' and was surprised at how calm her voice sounded.

'Holly.' It was David. 'Your father is being moved to Intensive Care now.'

So he wasn't dead. 'Did everything go all right?' Hope filled her voice.

David recognised it and groaned inwardly. Many times he had heard that tone in a relative's voice, and each time it became more difficult to destroy that hope. This time it was doubly so.

'Come down to Intensive Care,' he said gently. 'We'll talk there.'

Holly knew he was going to tell her that her father would not recover; otherwise he would have spoken more encouragingly. She was still holding the receiver, even though David had rung off.

'Oh, Angie.' Her voice was reed-like.

Angie took the receiver from her and replaced it. 'He's not. . .?' She couldn't say 'dead'.

'No, but David didn't sound hopeful. He wants to see me in Intensive Care.'

'I'll come with you,' Angie offered.

'No, thanks.' Holly placed a hand on her friend's arm. 'I'd rather go alone.'

'Well, you know where to find me,' said Angie gently.

David was standing beside her father's bed when she entered the intensive care unit. His shoulders were bowed, his expression brooding. The eyes he turned to her were defeated. There was no need for him to speak. She set aside her grief and thought of him. There must be nothing worse for a surgeon than to know he had failed.

'I know you did your best.' Words of comfort came easily to her lips. She longed to put her arms about him, kiss his distress away. 'No one could have done more.' She put her hand on his arm. He placed his larger one over it and they stood looking into each other's eyes, giving and receiving comfort.

It lasted but a moment, this communion between them. She turned to look down at the familiar, yet strange man in the bed and sat beside the recumbent figure, taking his limp hand in hers.

'I wish I'd not wasted those years.' She could tell David what she had not been able to tell Angie.

The face she raised to his had lost its youth; it had matured. Deep sadness dwelt in her eyes.

What could he say? How could he comfort her? What words would allay her suffering?

'You mustn't torment yourself.' It was hard to keep emotion from his voice, she moved him so. There was a melancholy beauty about her honed, pale face, haloed by auburn curls. 'You made your father very happy; he told me so when I met him at the club one day.' It wasn't really a lie. David had spoken to Mr Grant, had observed a lightness in the older man's step, noticed how much more relaxed his face was.

The eagerness in her face caught at his heart and he

wished he could lift this time for her, shoulder her grief, smooth the path that lay ahead, but he knew she had to travel it alone. He had already been there, years ago, but he had had a distraction. He had had Mike to look after. All he could do was to stay with her.

He watched her lean forward, and heard her low voice say, close to her father's ear, 'I love you, Dad.'

Watched her squeeze his hand and stroke his face, and felt like an intruder, but did not want to leave her alone.

Holly felt David's presence, but the whole of her being was concentrated on her father. She willed him to hear her words, but he made no sign, just sank deeper and deeper into unconsciousness until he slipped away as death claimed him.

'Holly.' David touched her arm. 'Come away.'

'D'you think he heard me?' she implored. 'D'you think he knew I was here?'

It was almost too much for him. 'Yes.' There was a tremor in his voice. He controlled it with an effort. 'I'm sure he knew.' He drew her to her feet. 'You know that hearing is the last sense to die.'

His words consoled her. 'Thank you, David.'

He led her away. 'You were getting on so well lately. Take comfort from that.'

'Yes.' She brightened a little. 'We had a super holiday.'

Suddenly, pictures of her father sitting in the sun, laughing and happy, so very much alive, such a contrast to the man lying silent and still in the bed, flashed before her eyes, and a sob, more pathetic because it was muted, escaped her.

David put his arm round her shoulders and drew her into an empty side-ward. He sat beside her on the bed and let her cry, holding her in a gentle embrace, dabbing her wet face with his handkerchief. It took a great deal of will-power to stop his own tears falling.

Gradually she quietened. She turned a face pinched with exhaustion towards him. 'Thanks again, David.' A last sob caught in her throat. She tried to smile. 'You're always rescuing me.'

He pulled her close and kissed her wet cheeks.

'That's what friends are for—to be there when needed.'

But I need you all the time, a voice cried inside her. Holly rose from the bed, turning away from him so that he wouldn't see how he added to her vulnerability.

He came and stood beside her. 'I'll take you home,' he said gently.

As they walked along the corridor he asked her if she would be all right on her own at Sheeplaw.

'Yes.' Her face was composed; even a little colour had returned to her cheeks. 'The house is also my friend.'

He drove carefully; sheep sometimes strayed on to the road. Headlights caught glowing eyes as he swung round corners. It was eerie, ghostly, and she shivered and was glad when David drew up outside her home.

Holly put the key in the lock and was suddenly afraid. She felt David's hand on her elbow as she hesitated. She knew he understood how she felt and was grateful for his support. The door swung wide and they entered together.

The essence of her father still lingered in the hall. His old jacket was hanging on the hall stand. His walking stick with its wolf's head gleamed in the corner, old gumboots for rough weather stood beside it as if waiting for their owner to climb into them.

They went into the lounge. Her ears seemed to be listening, her eyes searching. She felt her father's presence in the room with them.

'I'll make some coffee.' David's voice shocked her. Its timbre was so similar to her father's that it was as if the dead man had spoken.

It was an effort for her to control her imagination, but she managed it and said, 'We'll make it together,' and even managed to smile.

David was pleased to see the calmness in her face. He had been worried that returning to her home, with its memories, might upset her more, but it seemed to have helped her.

In the kitchen, as she filled the kettle and reached for the mugs, she thought of that time following the swimming episode.

He was thinking of it, too, as he watched her hands move, watched her hair fall over her cheeks as she bent her head; the copper curls were not so bright now. He watched the turn of her shoulder, the line of her neck, and was moved immeasurably. He wanted to touch her, comfort her, caress her, but knew he wouldn't. Now was not the time.

Holly made the coffee and David carried the tray into the lounge. She had almost finished hers when he said, 'Would you like me to see to the arrangements?'

She would very much have liked his help but knew she wouldn't be able to cope with seeing so much of him, so said, 'That's kind of you to offer, but I have an uncle in Edinburgh, Dad's brother, who will see to everything.'

'Good.' He rose and looked down at her. They had lit the fire when they'd come into the room, and its glow caught her hair, giving it back some of its sparkle.

She went with him to the door.

'If you need me for anything. . .' He reached for her hand.

Need him? If only he knew how much. 'You've been very kind, but I'm sure I'll manage.' She withdrew her hand. 'I'll recommend you as a counsellor.' She gave him a wan smile.

'If I need a reference I'll ask you.' He smiled. Suddenly the urge to feel her in his arms, her body close to his, became too strong. He reached out and enfolded her, but his emotions were tinged with sadness. She had Andrew and he—he had his commitment to Christine. This dear girl in his arms was out of reach.

David's jacket smelt like her father's, and tears fell afresh, but silently, poignantly. He produced another handkerchief. 'For damsels in distress I always keep two.'

She smiled tremulously. Her courage was one of the things he found so endearing.

The phone rang. Holly did not want to leave his comforting embrace, but she must. It was Andrew.

'I've just heard,' he said. 'I'm terribly sorry. Is there anything I can do?'

'Not at the moment, Andrew, thanks. But if you phone tomorrow.' She was using him as a shield between herself and David, whose presence behind her she was so aware of.

'Take care of yourself, Holly,' Andrew said.

She replaced the receiver and looked at David. His face was expressionless, and yet she felt he was hiding behind its impassivity.

'I'm sure Andrew will be very sympathetic.' He hadn't meant it to sound sarcastic—it was his jealousy talking.

Holly hadn't heard the mockery in his voice. He just sounded as if he were glad to hand her over to Andrew.

'I'd better be going.'

He was the doctor once more. She even expected him to whip out a prescription pad, write on it, hand it to her and say, 'Take three times a day.' Where was the compassionate man? Had mentioning Andrew wrought the change?

Suddenly she wanted him to go. She wanted him to take the tension she was feeling away with him. At the front door, she said, 'I'll wash your hankie and return it.'

The street lights hardened his features, making it stern and forbidding. Then he smiled, but it looked like a smile given involuntarily, as if he had not wanted it there on his face, but could not stop it.

'Take care of yourself,' he said, using Andrew's words unknowingly.

The SNO gave her a few days' compassionate leave. Her uncle and aunt came down from Edinburgh. She was glad to be able to leave the funeral arrangements to them.

The autumn leaves, yellows, green and tan, brightened the newly turned earth at the graveside that cold October day of her father's funeral. Holly raised her eyes and met David's; they were filled with compassion. He was standing with Christine among the other mourners—friends and colleagues of her father. David was taller than any of them, even taller than her uncle. A slight breeze blew the dark, almost black hair across his forehead. Lifting a hand, he brushed it aside. He stood straight-backed, head up, unconsciously assuming a fearless pose, and she loved him more than ever. Christine Nicol, smart and sophisticated in a grey suit, her classical features set in sympathetic lines, had her arm through his.

A voice beside her broke through her misery. 'If there's anything I can do. . .' It was Andrew.

'Thanks you, D——' she nearly said 'David', he was so in her thoughts '——Andrew. Everything seems to be under control.' Except for my traitorous heart, it whispered.

But she was grateful for his solid dependability.

'I'll always be your friend,' he said, and she was relieved to hear sincerity in his voice; he really meant 'friend', and she took his arm.

David watched them. They looked right together.

'Come on, Christine,' he said. 'We'd better say goodbye.'

Holly was standing with her uncle, her hand on Andrew's arm.

'We can't come to the house,' Christine explained. 'I'm due back on duty and David has to see a patient.'

She sounds like a wife, thought Holly, and said, 'I understand.'

David didn't say anything, just smiled.

Holly watched their elegant figures pick their way through the gravestones.

'We'd better go as well,' her uncle said. 'We must be at the house before the others.'

'Yes,' she said, but continued to watch David open the passenger-door for Christine.

He must have been aware of her looking in his direction, for he raised a hand in salute before he took his place beside Christine.

CHAPTER EIGHT

MR BRADY was still a patient on the ward when Holly returned to duty. He was a constant reminder of her loss. She tried to treat him as just another patient, but could not prevent herself from being stiff and unnatural when she took his temperature. The other patients knew he was the cause of her father's death and ignored him. He had recovered from his concussion and tried to apologise, saying, when she removed the thermometer from his mouth, 'I'm sorry.' His face was creased with distress. 'I'd lost my job—been made redundant—and drank too much.'

She should have felt compassion for him but felt nothing. This worried her greatly. She did not know what to say to him, so just gave him a weak smile and moved to the next bed.

The police were charging him with manslaughter and she felt nothing about that either. She just seemed to be numb.

During the next few weeks Holly struggled with her grief and remorse. She tried to take comfort from David's words, those he had spoken when her father had died, but, whenever she entered the house, memories of past quarrels concerning her choice of career rose like ghosts.

She lost weight, the sparkle went from her eyes, and her confidence was slipping. It was as if she were a different person. Work was her consolation. She stayed on duty longer than was needed and arrived well before the others.

Towards the end of November, Christine took two

weeks' holiday. Holly was in the treatment-room, checking the cupboards, when David came in. She glanced up at him enquiringly, a packet of cling bandages in her hand.

'I want to talk to you, Holly.' He took the bag from her and put it away, his movements as decisive as his voice.

Her mind reviewed his cases rapidly, but could think of nothing she had missed. Being in charge of the ward was a great responsibility and, because of her unsure state, she had double-checked everything.

David examined her strained face with professional interest. 'Are you sleeping?'

Irritation flashed in her eyes. He was like all the others—her friends and even Christine, constantly asking her how she was, even suggesting she took a few days off.

'Yes,' she answered shortly, turning back to the cupboard.

He had seen her anger, and smiled a little. This was more like the old Holly, though he suspected she was not telling him the truth. Perhaps he had the answer to her problem, so he said, 'You're a great one for upholding causes, aren't you?' he asked.

His words were so unexpected that she turned too quickly to face him and knocked a bag of savlodil to the floor. He bent to pick it up and handed it to her. He was pleased to see curiosity livening her sad eyes.

'So?'

'If you're interested I'll pick you up at seven-thirty and tell you all about it.' He smiled at her astonishment that he should know she was off. 'I asked one of the girls,' he explained.

Since the funeral Holly had come to accept that David was in love with Christine. The tension she had always felt in his presence had left her and she found she could behave naturally with him. Her awareness of him sexually was still there, but tempered now, so she could say, 'Setting tongues wagging again?' as a joke, made without a deeper meaning.

He grinned, enjoying the banter and riposte, 'Of course. Must keep the gossips happy.' He turned with his hand on the doorknob. 'I promise not to appear in jeans.'

'Formal tonight, then, is it?'

'Yes.' He winked. 'Best bib and tucker.'

'But won't you tell me what it's about?'

'Must keep you in suspense. Add zest to the evening.'

She moved towards the door and he opened it for her.

He strode away. A shaft of winter sunshine held him in its beam for a moment. How she wished she could be that beam.

Mrs Braithwaite was still at the house when Holly arrived home at six-thirty. She fussed around her late employer's daughter. 'I've made a small casserole for you, lass. You've only to pop it in the microwave.'

Holly did not tell her that she was going out, just thanked her, adding, 'You shouldn't have waited,' as she helped the grey-haired lady into her coat, noting how worn it was. Mrs Braithwaite was a widow, who must, by now, be a pensioner. It seemed as if the older woman had always been there. Mr Grant had left her an annuity and Holly hoped a new coat would be a priority purchase. If it wasn't Holly would buy her one.

'Now you make sure you eat your supper, Miss Holly,' said Mrs Braithwaite as Holly saw her away at the front door.

'I will,' she promised.

Since her father's death Holly had not bothered about her appearance, flopping about in jeans and sweatshirt when she was off. She had refused all invitations to go out, preferring to tramp on the moors or watch television.

But this evening she opened her wardrobe and drew out a dark green wool dress that had long sleeves, round neck and a fitted bodice that flattered her figure, making her full bust seem smaller. It had been too tight for her in the past, but now fitted her perfectly.

Normally she wore a little make-up, but this evening she applied some colouring to her pale cheeks and used a brighter lipstick.

Her hair had been neglected and was quite long. When on duty she wound it up and fixed it under her cap, and when off in a pony-tail. Tonight she brushed and brushed it until it shone. A smile lightened the sombreness of her face when she saw how alive it looked, and wished it reflected how she felt.

She fixed a gold brooch of ancient design that had been her mother's to the shoulder of the dress and slipped her feet into black suede shoes. She took a beige fur jacket from the wardrobe and ran her hand over its smoothness; it was so realistic for nylon.

The doorbell rang. Was it seven-thirty already? A glance at her watch confirmed it. Picking up a black envelope bag, she hurried downstairs. A memory of that previous time when she had had to change caught at her, and she half expected to hear her father's voice from the lounge. She suppressed a sob and opened the door. David was standing there, looking so handsome in dark grey suit, grey shirt and navy tie that her heart contracted.

He drew in his breath sharply. There was a luminous quality about her, a depth to her grey eyes. Her weight-loss had transformed her from a young woman, with vestiges of puppy fat, to a woman, still young but with the figure of a model and the assurance of one older than her years.

He smiled broadly. 'Well, there's my lovely, then,' he said in a broad Yorkshire accent.

She laughed. 'Rather a backhanded compliment, Mr Consultant Quinn,' she teased. 'It sounds as if you're referring to your pet cow.'

He grinned and took her arm, leading her to the car.

They drove towards Harrington. As they drew nearer the sky over the town glowed from electric light.

Holly wondered where he was taking her. He turned off before they reached the town, and shortly afterwards swung left into a circular drive, the car's wheels crunching on the gravel.

'Hammond Hall!' Holly exclaimed as she recognised the large square building illuminated by spotlights. It was stone-built, solid and imposing.

'You know it?' he asked, helping her out of the car.

'Yes. I thought it was going to become a museum.' She hitched her jacket more firmly on to her shoulders. 'I didn't know it was still a hotel.'

He didn't answer. They entered through a large door. A man of medium height, stockily built, approached them.

'Mr Quinn.' He greeted David with deference.

Holly knew him by sight; he was the owner-manager, Mr Stevens. She was impressed.

'We've followed your instructions,' he said as they walked beside him across the parquet floor. 'Would you like a drink first?' He gestured towards the bar just visible through an open door.

Holly was intrigued. What instructions?

'Yes.' David smiled. There was something more in his smile than politeness. These two men knew each other. Perhaps Mr Stevens had been a patient.

The room they entered was square. Burning logs in

the grate of a large fireplace scented the air. The bar faced it.

Holly stretched her hands out towards the blaze and turned a face alive with happiness in David's direction. 'It feels like Christmas,' she said, the firelight haloing her red hair.

He wished he could keep her like that forever, relaxed, happy and glowing. He caught one of her hands; it was warm and soft. 'What would you like to drink?'

'I don't know. Surprise me.'

She slipped off her jacket and seated herself in a comfortable, worn leather chair beside the fire and looked about her. There were few people at the bar. David wouldn't have to wait to be served. A couple at a table, near to where she was sitting, were holding hands. She tried not to look at them, they were so obviously in love.

A yearning to be loved like that swept over her. She looked up and saw the one who could fulfil this desire approaching. Her expression was sombre and he mistook it for grief.

He took a seat in the chair beside her and said, 'That will put some colour in your cheeks,' placing a medium-dry sherry on the table between them.

She lifted her glass in salute and smiled. He took a sip of whisky and, as he did so, glimpsed the young couple.

'Ain't love grand?' he said, grinning at Holly.

'Sometimes.' Her tone was weary.

'Having trouble with your love-life?' His face was set in sympathetic lines.

'In a way,' she said cryptically.

'Maybe I can help.' He sounded very willing.

She smiled at that. 'I'll let you know if you can.'

He took both her hands in his. 'I will do anything to make your life easier.' His expression was intense.

He was only being kind, she knew, and she appreciated it. There was such a good relationship between them these days that she didn't want to spoil it. If he kept hold of her hands and looked at her so affectionately she knew she would not be able to keep her love for him from showing in her eyes. If this happened it would be impossible for her to remain at Harrington General, and she did not want to leave. She couldn't bear not to see him again.

She pulled her hands away and reached for her glass. 'You seem to be well known here,' she said to divert him.

'It's the first time I've dined here.' There was a subtle change in his face.

'Is the owner a friend?' She blushed when she realised how blunt that sounded.

He laughed.

'Sorry. I didn't mean to be inquisitive.' She smiled.

'That's all right. He is a friend, in a way.'

A waiter approached them. 'Your table's ready, sir.'

The dining-room was of moderate size, panelled in dark wood; slightly shabby blue velvet drapes hung either side of tall windows. The carpet was of similar colour; threadbare patches were inadequately concealed beneath the tables. It would appear that the hotel was losing money.

The meal, however, was excellent. They started with fresh salmon, followed by roast spiced fillet of beef, aubergine rings and baby potatoes, finishing with strawberry pavlova. David chose a wine to complement the meal, but only tasted it, as he was driving.

'I wouldn't have minded fruit juice,' she said.

'Oh, no.' He shook his head. 'You're my guest, and, besides, I'm trying to soften you up.'

Holly had forgotten he had invited her for a reason, she had been enjoying herself so much.

'Am I softened up enough now?' She smiled, wishing the meal could go on forever.

The lighting in the dining-room was muted and she was grateful for this. The wine had relaxed her and she was afraid he would see how much she cared for him.

'We—ell.' He pretended to assess her, his eyes twinkling, his face amused. 'Not quite. Maybe coffee and a liqueur will do the trick.'

She laughed. 'I don't think you need to go that far.'

'Let's have our coffee in the lounge and see.' He reached for her hand and drew her to her feet.

He tucked her arm through his. For someone who had said he didn't know the hotel, David seemed very familiar with its layout, for he led her without hesitation to the lounge. Why had he deceived her? Uncertainty gripped her as she preceded him. This room also needed refurbishing. The green drapes were worn at the edges; the velvet had lost it nap. The green carpet was showing signs of wear and the patterned suite was faded in parts.

Holly was puzzled. The run-down atmosphere of the hotel didn't fit with David's sophistication.

The waiter brought their coffee and placed it on a low table. Holly looked at David. 'Black or white?' she queried.

'Don't tell me you've forgotten,' he teased.

She pretended to think, then said, 'Black,' and smiled. 'With one sugar.'

He laughed and accepted his cup.

They were alone in the lounge. He looked at her, a quizzical expression on his face. 'You're wondering why I brought you here.'

'Mind-reader.'

His face became serious. His whole demeanour changed.

'I wanted you to see the house because the friend who has bought it is thinking of turning it into an AIDS hospice.' So that was why Mr Stevens was familiar with David.

She was so surprised that she just stared at him. A friend had bought a house? She remembered David and Christine looking at houses. Was this the result?

He was watching her through narrowed lids. 'Yes, this is the house.' He had guessed what she was thinking. 'Christine is the buyer.'

Holly recovered quickly. 'I see.' And she did. This house was obviously not a love-nest, but that did not mean that David wasn't going to marry Christine.'

Holly concentrated on the idea of a hospice. 'I think it's a great idea.' She lifted the coffee-pot and looked at him enquiringly. When he shook his head she poured some for herself. 'How can I help?' Her eyes were bright with interest.

He smiled at her enthusiasm, pleased that his idea of recruiting her had succeeded. 'By coming to a meeting. I'll explain.' His face was earnest. 'The local authority agreed that the house could be bought and used as a hospice. The sale went ahead and plans for the conversion were approved.' He shrugged. 'But now the local people are objecting. They say that they don't want an AIDS hospice on their doorstep.' A smile broke out on his face. 'But we're going to convince them. We're holding a meeting in Harrington Town Hall on Wednesday evening. I hope you'll be able to come and bring with you as many people as you can.'

'I'll do my best.'

'The vet school owes you a debt—perhaps you can persuade some of the students to support us.' His tone was light, but the expression in his eyes didn't match it; they were tense.

'I'm seeing Andrew tomorrow, so I'll ask him.'

'D'you see a lot of him?' She sensed he really wanted to know and wondered why.

'Now and again.' She did not elaborate. Her tone was a little stiff, and he thought it was because he was being inquisitive.

A coolness had sprung up between them. She didn't want that. She didn't want anything to spoil their friendship, so she smiled at him and said, 'I can't see why anyone should object to an AIDS hospice here,' hoping to lead him away from personal subjects. 'It's not even near the town.'

'No, neither can I.' He seemed eager to accept the change of subject. 'But I suppose it's because it's within walking distance and the people who live near by don't want to have any contact with the patients who will still be able to walk to the shops.'

'How ridiculous.' She frowned with anger. 'I don't know how people can think like that. Don't they realise how dreadful it must be to know you have full-blown AIDS, to know you haven't long to live?' Compassion swept the anger from her eyes.

'I don't think they do. The majority of the general public don't see sickness and death the way we do.' His eyes reflected her pity. 'The tragedy is that so many of the patients are young. It's heartbreaking.'

There seemed to be more behind his words than concern for the victims of AIDS, he was so intense, so earnest. She wondered how he had become involved.

He guessed what she was thinking. 'A friend of mine has AIDS,' he explained. 'It's an old story. He had an affair with a woman when he was working abroad.' His eyes were sad, and she could have wept for him.

'I'm sorry,' she said, reaching out to touch his arm.

He smiled, though his eyes remained sombre. 'You have a tender heart, Holly, my love.' It was said lightly, without meaning, but oh, how she wished he had meant it.

'Time we were going,' he said, reaching for her hand and pulling her to her feet. They were inches apart. He seemed to be studying her.

'Looking for something?' she said with a cheeky grin.

'Maybe.'

Holly sensed a desolation in him and placed a hand on his chest as if, by doing so, she would soothe his troubled heart. David put his arms around her and drew her close. He touched her lips with his; it was light and fleeting. Then he released her, and she did not know what an effort it cost him.

'We must go,' he said, and his voice was rough.

His kiss, which could hardly have been called a kiss, had stirred her suppressed passion. It was so strong that she trembled. She was glad the waiter was approaching to distract David.

Holly was tense on the journey home and spoke little. He, too, was quiet. When they arrived she asked him in for coffee out of politeness, hoping he would say no, and when he did was perversely disappointed.

'Thanks for a lovely dinner,' she said.

He smiled. 'Even though it had an ulterior motive?'

She wanted to say, I don't care what the motive was. Just being with you, watching the expressions cross your face; how the light alters the colour of your eyes; feeling the touch of your hand; being near to you: these things mean everything to me.

Her feeling gathered speed so quickly that they came out as words, and she said impulsively, 'Does there have to be a reason for us to see each other?'

The shock of her reply stunned him for a moment, then he said, 'What about Andrew?'

She felt like answering, What about him? I'm not interested in him, I'm interested in you, but said, 'What about Christine?'

His whole demeanour changed. He frowned and, to Holly, he looked stern, and she felt awful, as if she had thrown herself at him. Opening the car door, she fled.

'Holly!' he called. But she had her key in her hand and quickly let herself into the house and leant against the closed door, her cheeks burning, her heart beating in time with the footsteps she heard approaching. The bell rang. There was a knock on the door level with her head.

'Holly,' he called, but she was too ashamed to face him, and remained silent.

His footsteps receded; his car drove away. How would she be able to face him on the ward? But she did not have to. The registrar took the rounds next day.

'David's been asked to chair an AIDS conference,' he explained.

Over the next few days Holly devoted herself to searching out those who had helped either to sponsor or take part in the recent events. She persuaded them to support the meeting. Some of her colleagues responded immmediately, but others were against the idea.

She left the canteen with one of the nurses and was appalled to hear the girl, a third-year student, say 'I wouldn't want an AIDS hospice near where I live.'

'Why?' A dangerous light flickered in Holly's eyes.

'Well. . .' The nurse shrugged. 'You know. . .'

Holly raised her eyebrows. 'No. Do tell.'

Her sarcasm was lost on this particular girl.

'Well. . . I might catch it.'

Holly let out a slow breath. 'Catch it? Don't be ridiculous. You can't catch it by speaking to someone, or sitting beside, or touching a person who has AIDS.' She was shocked at the young woman's ignorance. 'Don't you read any of the information circulated about AIDS? Don't you attend any of the lectures?' Holly was very angry.

The nurse took a step backwards and made to move away. Holly caught hold of her arm.

'Tell me.' Her face was flushed; her red hair seemed to glow as angrily. 'If a patient came to your ward and was HIV positive, wouldn't you care for them?'

A smug expression appeared on the nurse's face. 'I'm in Out-patients. The question doesn't arise.'

'Oh? Out-patients is immune to AIDS?'

The quietness of Holly's tone, in contrast to her previous anger, made a greater impression on the nurse, who frowned. 'But. . .'

Holly didn't wait to hear what she had to say; she was already walking away. That'll give her something to think about, she thought grimly, her mind seething.

'Something upset you, Staff?' David's voice came from behind her.

Holly turned to face him, spots of anger still on her cheeks. She was so consumed with disgust at her colleague's attitude that she forgot how David and she had parted, and said, 'I've just heard such a piece of ignorance and prejudice about AIDS that I'm appalled.' Holly looked vital; her colour had returned, her hair was shining. It was good to see her so alive, and David smiled. 'And that woman was a nurse.'

They were walking up the corridor. The grey November day made his white coat seem even brighter.

'I know.' He had heard it all before. 'That's why we have got to educate people, and the meeting's geared to that end.'

'Well, you can count on me and quite a few others.'

He smiled. 'I knew I could.' He stopped outside the pharmacy. 'I must leave you here.'

She had taken only two steps when he called her back. His face was serious as he said, 'Holly, about Christine. . .'

It all came back then and she blushed. Before he could say any more she said, 'That's all right,' and backed away. 'There's no need to explain. I understand.' Turning, she hurried away, leaving David with a frustrated expression on his face.

Her blush had receded by the time she reached the ward corridor. She was about to turn in when Angie called from Women's Surgical and hurried to catch her.

'Mike and I are having a little party on Wednesday. It's just a bring-a-bottle do. Can you come?' She added slyly, 'Andrew's coming.'

'Look, Angie.' Holly was annoyed. 'Stop pairing me with Andrew. We're just good friends.' No wonder David thought the young vet meant something special to her if Mike told him so.

'Sorry,' Angie apologised. 'But Andrew does see quite a bit of you and we thought. . .'

Holly's annoyance increased. 'We just go out occasionally; apart from that we have the same friends, so naturally we are in the same company.'

'Does Andrew know you feel like that?' Angie was looking at her friend doubtfully.

'Of course he does. I told him.'

'Well, perhaps you'd better tell him again,' said Angie, a wry expression on her face.

Holly asked apprehensively, 'Why?' What has he been saying?'

'Nothing really.' Angie hurried to reassure her. 'It's just. . .' she frowned, trying to think of how to express what she felt '. . .an impression, I suppose.' She shrugged. 'Anyway, will you come?'

Holly would have liked to say no, having heard what Angie had said, but she was off. Then she remembered the meeting. 'I'd love to, but I'm going to the meeting at Harrington Town Hall that night—aren't you?'

'Yes, but the party is after that, about nine o'clock.'

So Holly accepted and they parted.

After reporting to Sister, Holly went into the ward and was just in time to grab a bowl and hold Billy Watson's head as he was about to vomit; he had had an emergency appendicectomy that morning. He was only sixteen and this was his first time in hospital. Lying back, exhausted and pale, he moaned, 'Oh, it hurts.'

'I know,' she murmured soothingly as she bathed his forehead with a damp cloth and moistened his dry lips. 'I'll get you something to ease the pain.'

When Holly entered the office Christine looked up from the treatment book. The ward sister looked tired and thin.

'Billy's in pain,' Holly explained.

Christine pulled his case notes forward and flicked them open. 'He can have his post-op now.'

She rose and reached into her pocket for the poison-cupboard keys, then looked enquiringly at Holly. 'Did I give the keys to you?' she asked as her hand came away empty, an anxious expression on her face.

'No.' Holly's face tightened.

They stared at each other in consternation. To lose the dangerous-drug cupboard's keys was disastrous, and Holly was surprised. Christine was so particular. It was so unlike her.

'They must be on the desk,' Holly said, darting forward to rifle among the papers. But they weren't.

Christine seemed unable to move. Her pale face was paler.

'Perhaps they've fallen in the basket,' she whispered. But no; there were only pieces of paper there.

'Have another look in your pocket,' Holly suggested.

Christine did, but shook her head mutely.

'What about the other one?' suggested Holly.

Christine delved her hand in, and out it came with the keys. Her face cleared, and they both breathed a sigh of relief. 'I never put them in that pocket so I didn't even think to look, and I suppose I didn't feel them because I've a tissue in there.' Her face had a strained look.

'David told me you were the one who bought Hammond Hall. Perhaps you are doing to much,' said Holly.

'Did he tell you why?' There was a closed look about Christine's face.

'No.' Holly had not thought that there might be a reason for Christine's philanthropy.

Christine relaxed.

'I'll make you a cup of tea,' said Holly when Christine made no effort to confide in her.

'No. That poor boy's waiting.' She unlocked the cupboard and checked the drug with Holly, who hurried away to administer it.

Afterwards, as she discarded the empty syringe, she wondered about Christine. The ward sister had made a few slips lately, just minor things—drugs not ordered, X-ray reports not obtained. She was not as efficient as she'd used to be. Something was troubling her, and Holly wondered if it had anything to do with the AIDS project.

CHAPTER NINE

WEDNESDAY evening was wet and cold. When Holly came off at six she hurried to the nurses' home to change in Angie's room. As the party was to be casual, she slipped on a black skirt, teaming it with a soft pink woollen jumper. She quickly ate a sandwich with a cup of tea; she wasn't going to faint this time.

It was raining as she left the hospital. Up went her umbrella, and she hoped her thin shoes would not be soaked through by the time she reached the town hall. The street lights made patterns that moved on the wet road as the slight wind ruffled the water. The traffic lights seemed brighter when she looked up at them.

Quite a few people were already assembled when Holly arrived. She could see David's commanding figure—he was talking to Irene on the rostrum.

Holly approached them, keeping her umbrella away from people's clothing. Mike and Angie saw her and waved.

'You should have left your brolly and trench coat in the cloakroom,' Angie said.

'Where is it?'

Angie was directing her when David said, 'Not so fast.'

Holly looked up into his face, and was relieved to find it smiling down at her in his old familiar way. She smiled back. 'What can I do for you?'

'Now that's a leading question.' He was teasing her. 'We've a place for you here.' He indicated a chair.

'Good,' she said perkily. 'I've a few things I'd like to say.'

'Oh, you are brave,' Irene said, looking at her with admiration.

Holly ignored this and went to hang up her coat.

The others were already seated when she returned. She took her place at the end of the table and glanced over the assembled company. Andrew was not there. Perhaps he wasn't coming. She must have another talk to him.

Promptly at seven-thirty David rose.

'As you know, this meeting, which I'm glad to see so well attended, has been organised to discuss the opening of an AIDS hospice, using Hammond Hall.' His face was serious as he continued, 'Tonight we hope to allay any fears raised by this project. In spite of the media coverage, people are still ignorant about how the disease is transmitted, many thinking it can be caught by ordinary contact. We plan to put this right tonight.' He paused. 'I'll commence by introducing the panel.'

After he had done so he explained how AIDS was contracted, and a lively discussion ensued, with agreements and disagreements flying backwards and forwards. The force of David's personality controlled the meeting.

'I still don't want anyone from one of these places coming into my shop,' a belligerent, red-faced, bull-like man shouted. 'I don't care what you say.' His outflung arm pointed directly at David. 'Why can't you have this hospice somewhere else? Or don't have it at all.'

'Would you like your son or daughter to have nowhere to go if they had AIDS? No one to give them special care?' Holly's voice rang out.

'My son and daughter wouldn't get this disease,' he shouted back, his expression affronted. 'They're clean young people. They don't use drugs or do. . .anything.' His face had reddened with embarrassment.

'I hope you're right,' said David quietly. 'It only takes one careless night.'

There was complete silence following his words. Then the discussion broke out again and continued until by nine o'clock nothing had been settled and the meeting broke up.

Holly felt drained. She was just stepping off the rostrum when Andrew appeared at her side.

'Sorry,' he apologised. 'Had to help Dad with a sick cow.'

Her smile was tight. 'That's OK. Are you going to Mike and Angie's party?'

'Yes. And you?'

Holly nodded. Andrew slipped his arm through hers. She tried to pull away but the crush of people was too great.

'Made it, I see.' David's voice came from behind them, its tone sarcastic.

Andrew and Holly turned their heads. What a single-minded man he was, thought Holly.

'Andrew was held up with a "sick patient",' Holly defended him.

She was telling him off. Rushing to her Andrew's defence. Was he her lover? David mused. Pain at the thought stiffened his face, hardened his eyes.

He doesn't have to look so fierce because one person missed the meeting, Holly thought, turning away with Andrew.

David followed them. They met up with Angie and Mike at the door. 'I've got your coat and umbrella,' her friend said.

'Thanks.' Holly took them from her and heard David say, 'I'll be along later, Mike. Have to collect Christine.'

Of course, thought Holly. She'd forgotten that the ward sister was on duty.

The rain had stopped, but the pavements were still wet. David's feet slap-slapped as he walked in the opposite direction.

As the door swung wide into Mike's flat, music greeted them. The party had already started. John bounded out of the lounge.

'Hi! Hope you don't mind us starting without you.' He didn't sound very apologetic.

Holly could see Mike was annoyed, but he covered it up very well. 'As long as you've left us something to eat,' he said.

'There's plenty of that.' One of the girls caught John's arm and pulled him back into the room.

Mike took the girls' coats. 'I'll put them in the bedroom. You two go into the lounge.'

It was a large room with a big bay window. Quite a few students were there with their girlfriends. Holly saw Janet Roberts and waved. Drinks were pressed upon them—a punch concoction. Holly wrinkled her nose at its taste; there was too much alcohol in it for her.

They had only been there for half an hour when Holly knew she shouldn't have come. She circulated, chatted here and there, then found a corner and sat down. Conversation buzzed over her head—'Did you know Dr Williams is dating Maureen?' 'Did that road accident come to your ward?' 'Sister wouldn't give me my holidays.'

You could never escape, thought Holly. Even when they were off duty, hospital life dominated them. Glasses clinked. Beer cans clattered. She became more and more tired. Her head started to ache. Her eyes kept swivelling towards the door as she waited for David to appear. It wasn't until ten-thirty that she turned her head and saw him standing with Christine. They had just arrived.

From that moment on the party held meaning for Holly. His presence acted like a tonic, reviving her. She rose from her seat and found she was standing beside Andrew. She had not seen much of him during the evening.

'So that's where you've been hiding,' he said. There was perspiration on his brow.

'Why don't you take your jacket off?' she suggested.

He obeyed her, and she took it from him. It was this wifely gesture that David saw. Holly watched Mike push towards his brother. David was still formally dressed, while Christine's two-piece was simple but expensive, navy blue with a small white spot, and a white fur jacket hung on David's arm.

A subtle change came over the party. The arrival of the consultant and ward sister had the effect of unwelcome parents, but it didn't last for long. Too much beer and punch had been consumed.

Holly listened with only half an ear to what Andrew was saying; she was studying David, trying to guess what he was talking about.

'Holly!' The sharpness in Andrew's voice brought her back.

'Sorry.' She gave him an enquiring look.

'I was only asking if you wanted another drink.' He sounded annoyed.

'Yes, please.' She smiled at him, ignoring his peeved expression. 'I could eat a sausage roll, too, if there are any left.'

Partly mollified by her smile, he went to carry out her request.

Holly's eyes swung back to where David had been. He was not there. Anxiously, she looked for him and found him almost at her elbow. Christine was not with him.

Holly felt weak with sudden desire and leant against

the wall, her heart beating so quickly that she thought she would suffocate. His nearness was so overpowering that she was unable to hide her awareness of him. She raised a hand, as if to ward him off, but he took it in his, his blue eyes searching her face.

'Holly?' His voice was husky, questioning.

It was as if they were alone in the room. Her ears were deaf to the music; she saw only him. Her hand trembled.

'Holly.' His voice caressed her name, his eyes were gentle. 'I. . .'

'I was lucky. Just got the last sausage roll.' Andrew's voice cut between them like a surgeon's knife.

David dropped her hand. 'I had my eye on that,' he said, his tone light.,

'I brought it for Holly,' Andrew said, tight-lipped.

David bowed and gestured for her to take it. 'Ladies first,' he said, his eyes twinkling.

She was not amused. 'You take it.' He made her emotions swing so—one moment she was happy, the next depressed. She felt like screaming at him. . .she felt like throwing herself into his arms. She felt like kicking him, then she felt like kissing him. So her voice sounded cross.

'Feeding on love?' He was mocking her.

'Yes, she is,' said Andrew, and pulled Holly into his arms and kissed her. There was no hesitation about him this time.

Holly was taken by surprise and was passive in his embrace for a moment, and during that moment David moved away.

Her distress at knowing Andrew had given the wrong impression gave Holly strength. She pushed him away.

'Why did you say that?' She was furious. 'Why did you kiss me?'

'Couldn't help it.' His voice was low. 'I love you.'

Her anger left her.

'It just came to a head.' He tried to explain, and Holly understood only too well. 'I've been wanting to kiss you like that for weeks.'

'Oh, Andrew.' She knew how he must feel. Wasn't she similarly placed? 'I'm so sorry.' She put a hand on his arm, and David, turning at that moment, saw the expression on her face and mistook compassion for love.

'Are you all right?' Christine asked him. 'You look awfully pale.'

David took her arm. 'Just tired. I think we should be going.'

Holly saw him leave and Andrew saw her expression.

'You love him, don't you?' His eyes were as bleak as hers; he still held the plate with its one sausage roll in is hand.

'Yes.'

'Will you forgive me, Holly?' He offered her the plate. 'Peace offering?'

She laughed, glad to see he still had a sense of humour, and took the sausage roll.

He drove her home and kissed her cheek. Watching him drive away, she was filled with a great weariness and decided to ask for a week off. As she shut the front door and allowed the comforting ambience of the house to soothe her, she knew how she would spend it; she would decorate the rooms, give her home a new face, and perhaps she would be able to do the same for herself. Her father's death had left her financially independent; she could give up nursing if she wanted to, but she loved work too much. She would concentrate on her career and be a surgical ward sister—the very best; bury her feelings for David Quinn.

The SNO was sympathetic. 'Do you good to have some time off. I'm sure Sister Nicol will be able to spare you.' She smiled and it transformed her rather severe features. She must have been beautiful when she was younger, thought Holly. I wonder if a nurse will say that about me one day. The idea depressed her. 'Flu hasn't got its grip on us yet,' the SNO continued, 'so our staffing levels are adequate.'

When her friends heard her plans to redecorate and refurbish her house, they exclaimed, 'But this is the wrong time of year!'

'I don't see why. Any volunteers?'

There were excuses and a hasty exit made except by Angie, who said, 'I'll come on my day off. Wednesday suit you?'

'Fine. I'll even give you lunch.'

When the bell rang on that day Holly had on an old pair of jeans and one of her father's shirts, her hair was tied up in a scarf, and her face was freckled with emulsion. She had the roller in her hand as she opened the door. David Quinn stood on the steop.

'Heard you were wanting volunteers.' His grin broadened as he looked at her face. 'I like your make-up.'

Her fingers tightened on the roller handle, but this was the only sign she showed that his sudden appearance had shocked her.

'I'm thinking of marketing it,' she quipped. 'Hospital grapevine been at it again?'

'No. Angie told me she was coming to help today, but I persuaded her to let me come in her place, at least for the morning.' Hope that his reason for coming was because he wanted to be with her was squashed when he said, his face becoming serious, 'I thought it would give me a chance to discuss the AIDS hospice with you. See if you have any ideas.'

Her disappointment was acute, but she hid it behind a cheerful, 'Come in.' And she gestured towards the lounge.

The room looked different, stripped of its photographs and ornaments, the furniture covered with dustsheets. She placed the roller in the tray and looked him up and down. He was wearing grey trousers and black shirt covered by a black anorak. He was even more potent in these colours.

Holly swallowed. 'You're not exactly dressed for painting,' she said briskly. Action was the only solution to the effect he was having on her. 'Come with me.'

She led him upstairs, saying over her shoulder, 'You can wear a shirt of my father's, and there's a pair of trousers that should fit.'

He followed her into the master bedroom. She opened the wardrobe. Her father's suits and jackets hung just were he'd left them; the sleeves still held the impression of his elbows. He had never used aftershave or talcum, just anti-perspirant and a good soap, and their smell lingered. Quickly she pulled the trousers from the hanger and handed them to David. Then, reaching into the top drawer of the heavy mahogany tallboy, she drew out a shirt, pausing with it in her hands for a moment, sadness catching her once more, before handing it over.

'You can change in here,' she said, eager to leave the room with its memories, but it wasn't only the memories of her father that disturbed her; David, standing beside the bed with his hand on its rail, flustered her.

As she went downstairs she decided that the only way to cope with her feelings was to look upon David as the ward consultant.

When he reappeared she handed him a brush. 'If you climb the ladder and paint the edges I'll use the roller.'

'Yes, Staff,' he said, smiling cheekily.

Suddenly she felt at ease. His jesting had relieved

her tension. He moved the ladder over the unpainted wall and dipped the brush in the emulsion, tapped off the surplus and climbed the rungs.

'Why are you using white?' he asked.

'I wanted an illusion of lightness, airiness. White seemed just right. I intend to change the curtains and have the suite re-covered.' She looked up at him, her eyes smiling. 'I'm going to get a new carpet as well.'

He smiled affectionately. 'I'm glad to see your grief is lifting a little.

She sighed. 'I'm learning to cope with it.' She rested her roller on the tray. A few wet paint-spots lay on her cheeks like white tears.

He loaded the brush once more, and commenced to paint.

'You're not thinking of selling the house, then?'

'Oh, no.' Her tone was shocked. 'I love this house, and Sheeplaw. I intend to live here always.' She lifted the roller. 'And die here.' Swish, swish went the roller.

'Well not just yet, I hope, especially as there's so much decorating still to do.' He smiled down at her.

She laughed.

'What does Andrew think about that—will he want to live here?'

Holly stopped painting and looked at him. His brush was suspended, his face tense. Red spots of anger appeared on her cheeks.

'Andrew will never live here,' she said. 'I don't know what Angie and Mike have hinted, but, whatever it is, it's wrong. Andrew and I are friends; that's all.' She looked as if she would like to throw the roller at him.

'Sorry.' The tautness left his face and he smiled. He seemed pleased.

She smiled back, glad that any misunderstanding about her relationship with Andrew had been resolved.

They painted companionably for a short time, then she said, 'You wanted some ideas to help the hospice?'

Swish, swish went his brush, a few drops flicking her way.

'Hey! You don't need to be so generous.'

He grinned. 'Too much enthusiasm.'

'That's great, but could you control it a little?'

'I'll do my best.' He saluted with the brush.

She was delighted. He was such fun to be with.

'I wonder if you have any thoughts on how we can persuade the locals to accept the hospice.'

She ran the roller smoothly up the wall. 'As a matter of fact, I have.' She looked up at him. 'Those outbuildings in the grounds; how about converting them into shops and letting the patients' relatives serve in them? That way they'll feel more involved, feel they are helping their loved ones.'

When he didn't answer immediately she thought it was because her idea wasn't feasible, so said, 'No good?'

'I think it's a great idea. It's so simple that it stunned me.' He grinned down at her. 'What a clever girl you are.' He descended the ladder, brush in hand. 'And I know just the person to help with the alteration.'

'Mr Davis,' they said in unison.

Mr Davis was a joiner who lived in Sheeplaw. David had repaired his bleeding ulcer and he had been so grateful that he had told the surgeon, 'Any time I can do anything for you, just say the word.' Holly had been there at the time.

'And his brother's an electrician,' said Holly, a wide smile on her face.

'Better and better.' His grin matched hers.

'And I believe there's a cousin.' They both laughed.

'No wonder you want to live in Sheeplaw.' He

balanced the brush on the tin, then, taking her by the shoulders, said, 'Holly Grant, you're a marvel.'

She wished he had not touched her. She was all right if he didn't, but his hands on her shoulders set her skin aflame. She twisted away and rubbed the roller unnecessarily hard in the tray, loading it too heavily.

'Of course I am,' she quipped.

'Back to work, then?' She thought she heard disappointment in his voice. Perhaps he had planned on kissing her, and though she longed to feel his lips on hers she knew it would have increased her desire, and this she didn't want.

They carried on until one o'clock, with a small stop for coffee. The lounge was finished.

'Would you like to stay for lunch?' she asked, watching him clean the brush.

'Thanks, if it's not too much trouble.'

'No. It's the least I can do to repay you.'

'Oh, I can think of a better way.' His eyes were mischievous.

She laughed. 'I think you should keep that way for Sister Nicol,' she said, giving him a reproving look, which was only partly in jest.

He put the brush upside-down in the jam-jar and turned to her. 'There you go again, bringing in Christine. Why do you do it?' A frown of irritation drew his brows together. 'She is a friend who, at the moment, needs my help. It isn't for me to say why.' The eyes that looked at her were a doctor's eyes, used to keeping secrets. 'That's why you have seen me with her.' There was even a touch of sternness in his voice. 'But apart from that. . .' He didn't finish the sentence, but she knew he was telling her he was free emotionally, and she was suddenly shy.

She lowered her eyes. 'I'm afraid it's just soup and salad. Angie's dieting.'

Why was she talking like this? Why wasn't she throwing herself into his arms? Why was she acting as if his words held no meaning for her?

'That'll do fine.'

He had spoken naturally, and she glanced up at him, but his expression was stiff and she knew she had lost the moment. It was then that she realised that her unwillingness to openly show how she felt about him was because she was afraid of the intensity of her love, feared his love would be snatched from her. It was a backlash from her father's death, and she didn't know what to do about it. How to put it right. She had been given what she wanted and couldn't take it. Despair made her turn away, and it looked as if she had rejected him.

'So it's Andrew after all.' His face was bleak.

How could she say 'No, it's my father'? It would sound too ridiculous.

'I won't stay for lunch.' He moved towards the door. 'I'll just change.'

Holly heard him go upstairs, and waited in the hall for him.

'Goodbye, Holly,' he said when he came down, his face tight. It sounded as if it was forever.

She opened the door, too full of emotion to speak, but, as she stood on the step and watched him climb into his car, a whispered, 'Goodbye, my darling,' slipped from her lips.

She waited on the step until the car was out of sight, then went indoors, full of despair. What had she done?

Holly was washing the dishes mechanically when the rain started. She looked at the window. The rain was so heavy, and the wind so strong, that the drops ran into each other, and it looked as if a sheet of water was covering the window-pane.

She dried the dishes and put them away, then toured

the house, closing the windows. Holly was using her father's study as a lounge until the latter was refurbished. The room overlooked the moors, which spread, grey and bleak, wet and forbidding, a few yards from the garden. She shivered. The bleak landscape fitted in with the way she was feeling.

Quickly she bent to light the gas fire, hoping the brightness and warmth would take the cold from her bones. She was straightening when she heard the bell, and hurried to open it, hope flowing in her heart, thinking it might be David, but it was Andrew standing on the step, wet through.

'My car broke down a mile up the road.' His teeth were chattering and a whimpering sound came from inside his jacket.

'Come in,' she said, taking his arm and drawing him into the hall.

His shoes squelched, water dripped from his jacket, and his hair clung to his head, making it look smaller.

'I was bringing Shep back from the vet.' He exposed the bundle under his coat. A sheepdog puppy, its fur wet, its body trembling, looked up at her pathetically. 'Can I use your phone?'

'Of course you can, but I think you should have a hot bath and put on some dry clothes first. I'll give you some of my father's. They may be a bit big, but they'll do.'

'Thanks, Holly.' He surrendered the puppy into her arms and followed her up the stairs.

She drew a couple of towels from the linen cupboard, pulling an old one, at the same time, from the bottom shelf.

'The bathroom's there,' she said, handing him the towels. 'I'll pass you a dressing-gown and some clothes.'

He went into the bathroom. Holly wrapped the pup

in the old towel and held it close to her body, hoping her warmth would stop its shivering. Sorting through her father's clothes didn't affect her this time—she was in too much of a hurry; she wanted to put the puppy by the fire.

She knocked on the bathroom door and an arm came flapping out. She thrust the clothes into its grasp.

Downstairs, she rubbed the puppy dry, and was looking for an old piece of blanket in the kitchen cupboard when the bell went. She shut the puppy in the study and went to answer it.

At the same time that she opened the door to find David on the step, Andrew appeared at the top of the stairs, wearing her father's dressing-down. 'Holly,' he called.

The stairs faced the front door. The young vet, his hair tousled, was clearly visible.

There was a long, terrible silence. Holly's face froze into a death-mask, it was so bloodless. Only her eyes were wide with shock as she realised how David would interpret Andrew's half-naked appearance.

She was speechless, numb. And David. . .he just looked at her. Their silence was more expressive than words. Then a sigh escaped his lips. It was as if the wind had been let out of a balloon; he seemed to shrivel before her. He turned and left her. He didn't see her stricken face, her hurt eyes. She closed the door quietly.

'Is everything all right, Holly?' Andrew was descending the stairs. 'I was only going to ask for a face-cloth.'

The innocent catalyst was standing, looking like a young boy.

'I'll get you one,' she said, not answering his question, following him up the stairs.

She felt as if her life had ended.

CHAPTER TEN

OVER the next few days, when the pain and anguish had subsided to a level she could cope with, Holly became angry with herself and with David—with herself because she had not told him that she loved him, and with him because he had not waited for an explanation for Andrew's state of undress.

When she returned to duty Holly avoided David as much as possible. Christine usually did the ward rounds with him anyway, so this helped. If Holly glimpsed his sprawling figure in the office she would ask the junior nurse to fetch whatever she needed. He seemed to be making an effort to evade her as well.

On Tuesday, Holly was giving Mr Lawson, an old man scheduled for removal of melanoma from his left arm the next day, the operation consent form to sign. He had been admitted a week ago in a hotch-potch of clothes, looking undernourished and unkempt. Johnny Simpson had said, taking the case notes from her, 'Mr Lawson has a drink problem. David's not operating upon him until next week. He wants him fed on a high-protein diet to improve his resistance to infection.'

'I'll order it now.'

'I don't know how David managed to get the old devil to come in.' They had been in the office at the time. 'He's quite a character. You might have seen him trundling round the town centre, searching the waste bins.'

'I thought he looked familiar,' she said. Then she laughed. 'The girls had quite a job persuading him to have a bath, but he was no match for Sister.'

'No, I guess the ice maiden would put him in his place.'

Holly frowned. 'I wish you wouldn't call her that. She's not, you know. She's really caring.'

His eyebrows had risen. 'Pals now, are we?'

She had ignored his remark.

Holly caught the flash of white coats as she leant over Mr Lawson now. Glancing sideways, she saw David and Johnny approaching the bed.

'Where do I put my name?' Mr Lawson's voice was cross. He had difficulty writing at all.

Holly placed her finger beside the word 'signature'. 'Just there, Mr Lawson.'

Why did the doctors have to stand at the edge of her vision? She could feel David's eyes watching her. Mr Lawson seemed to be taking ages to scrawl his name.

Finally he was finished. She took the form from him and smiled. 'Thank you.'

The old man grinned back, and her smile broadened; he had such a cheeky face.

As she moved away she kept her face averted from the doctors. The glance she had taken had imprinted on her memory how the collar of David's white coat was turned up, that his hands had been in his pockets, that his trousers had knife pleats, his shoes were shining, and that he wore his university tie.

Holly sighed, and went to the office thinking that perhaps she should ask for a transfer to another ward, seeing David was breaking her heart.

She slipped the consent form into Mr Lawson's folder and wished she didn't have to attend the hospice meeting that evening.

As Mike was studying hard, Holly went with Angie.

'Let's have a pizza beforehand, shall we?' her friend suggested.

When they were seated Angie said, studying Holly

over the menu, 'How are you getting on?' She had not seen her friend for a while, and thought Holly was looking tired.

'Fine.' Holly didn't look up. She was deciding between lasagne and pizza.

'Stop hiding behind that menu and tell me what's wrong between you and David.' Her face was serious. 'He seemed very keen to see you. Made a special call to ask me if he could go in my place to help you paint.'

Holly lowered the menu. 'There's nothing wrong. His reason for coming was that he wanted to discuss the AIDS project.' Then she added sharply, 'Why? Has he said anything?'

'No, but he snaps every time we see him, and Mike heard him shout at a patient in the clinic.'

'Oh, that's nothing.' Holly raised the menu again. 'He often tells them off.'

'Only if there is a reason to,' Angie defended the consultant.

'Must we talk about him?' Holly was finding the subject distressing. It was bad enough that David should be constantly in her thoughts without having to talk about him as well. 'I wish they'd serve us.' She signalled to the waitress. The impatience Holly was feeling must have been obvious from her expression, for the young woman came over to them immediately to take their order.

'Has your sister decided on a theme for Christmas?' Holly asked, thinking this would be a neutral topic.

'For the ward, you mean?' And, at Holly's nod, she said, humouring her friend, 'It's a toss-up between a traditional scene and something more ambitious.' She smiled. 'I think the traditional will win.'

Discussion of the coming festivities lasted until the meal was over. Afterwards they made their way to the town hall. David was already there, talking to one of the councillors. He glanced in her direction and inclined his head in recognition, his face strained. She reciprocated. Neither of them smiled.

At seven-thirty the hall was full, and David rose. After the preliminaries he presented Holly's shop proposal. It reminded her of the happy time they had had painting together, and it was only by concentrating on the meeting that she was able to suppress her tears. Her ideas was received enthusiastically. It set the tone of the whole meeting, and by nine o'clock the AIDS hospice proposal had been accepted.

Holly glanced at David's face when the show of hands was almost unanimous; it was triumphant. He looked in her direction and she smiled; she couldn't help it, she was so pleased for him. The stiffness left his face, but he gave no answering smile.

At the end of the meeting Holly hung back, thinking it would be easier to leave when the main crush had thinned. Angie had already slipped out as Mike was expecting her.

David was delayed by one of the audience, who wanted a point clarified. Holly watched as the consultant explained patiently. She couldn't hear what was said, but envied the questioner David's smile.

The man David had spoken to was leaving the hall. Holly made to follow. David said from behind her, 'Andrew not here tonight?' His tone was sarcastic.

She turned to face him. 'No,' she said, and felt as if her heart was breaking. 'He's developed a chest infection. You see. . .' she was surprised how composed she sounded '. . .that evening you saw him in my father's dressing-gown his car had broken down and he had had to walk in the pouring rain, carrying a sheepdog pup in his jacket. He was wet through and needed a hot bath. Even so, it didn't prevent his getting a chill.' There was a simple dignity about the way she stood—upright, calm and beautiful.

He longed to take her in his arms, but she didn't want him, did she? 'I'm sorry,' he said, his voice contrite, his face stiff. 'I didn't——' But, before he could continue, Angie and Mike burst through the door.

'Thought we'd come back for you and invite you to the flat for a bite to eat,' Mike said. Then, looking at David, he added, 'What about you? Can you come?'

'No, thanks, Mike,' his brother said. 'Another time, perhaps.'

Christmas was coming. Holly did all the right things; decorated the ward, went shopping with one of the girls to buy presents to put in the stockings of those patients not well enough to go home. She even went to parties, but it was as if some other person were doing these things.

She caught David watching her, but he didn't approach. Professionally, they were polite.

On Christmas Day he came, as was the tradition, to carve the turkey. Christine tied the strings of his navy blue and white striped apron. He stood at the top of the ward, the large bird before him on a table, the patients' expectant faces turned to his, and said, holding out his hand, 'Scapel, Sister.'

Christine handed him the carving knife with a smile. Titters of appreciation came from the beds. Mr Lawson was the only patient fit enough to go home still left on the ward but, as he had no home to go to, they had kept him in. He passed out the plates. David had caught the old man swearing at Jean Bailey two days after his operation and Holly was told how David had said, 'Now, Harry. Remember what I told you. Any more discourtesy to the nurses and you won't be here for Christmas.'

Mr Lawson had been a changed man since.

There was a Christmas dance for the hospital staff on January the third. Holly had decided not to go, making as her excuse, 'I'd have to stay in Harrington overnight; it finishes too late for me to get home.' She was having a drink in the Surgeon's Arms at the time.

'That's no problem,' said Mike cheerfully. 'You can stay at my flat. John's gone home for Christmas.'

'Well. . .' She looked from Angie to Mike; both their faces were encouraging her. 'But I haven't a partner.' She had finally persuaded her friends that she was not involved with Andrew.

'That's no problem,' Angie said. 'I heard Johnny Simpson bemoaning the fact that his fiancée wasn't able to go because her mother is ill. I'm sure he'd love to partner you.' Angie thought a night out might brighten her friend's sad eyes.

Holly was trapped.

'Come on,' encouraged Mike. 'You can't let the side down. If there isn't a good attendance the powers that be might not put on a dance next year.'

Holly smiled. 'Put like that, how can I refuse?'

'I'll ask Johnny for you,' offered Angie to make sure that Holly could not back out.

The following day she was taking the last temperature when Johnny approached her. 'I hear I'm taking you to the dance,' he murmured.

Holly removed the thermometer from Kevin Law's mouth. He'd been admitted yesterday after his bicycle had skidded on the ice, tossing him off. He had severe grazes to arms and legs, which had needed scrubbing in Theatre under anaesthetic.

'Oooh, I wish I was in your shoes, Doc. Our Staff's a cracker.'

Johnny smiled down at the eighteen-year-old. 'Good job Staff's taken your temperature, young man, as thinking like that would have raised it.'

Kevin grinned.

'Breaking more hearts, Staff?' David's voice came from behind them. It was the first time he had spoken directly to her since the meeting.

Holly glanced up at the controlled face. Was he joking or being sarcastic? Kevin obviously thought it was the latter, for he rushed to defend the staff nurse he had a crush on. 'Nothing like that,' he said, and blushed.

David was looking at Holly. 'Someone else to your rescue, Miss Grant.' His voice had softened.

'But perhaps more worthy.' She hadn't meant to say that; it was her hasty tongue again, wanting to hit back for the hurt he had caused her.

His olive branch spurned, David said in a stiff voice, 'Perhaps we could do the round?'

'Of course.' Johnny jumped with alacrity.

Christine was pushing in the case-note trolley, helped by the students; it was to be a teaching round. As Holly made to pass her Christine said, 'I want you on the round this morning, Staff. I'm expecting the SNO to send for me.'

Holly noted Christine's tired eyes and wondered what was wrong. David knew but had felt unable to tell Holly, who had felt unable to ask.

Holly kept out of David's sight as much as possible during the round. When the phone rang Nurse Bailey hurried to answer it, returning quickly.

'Excuse me, Sister. The SNO wants to see you,' she said.

Christine glanced at David, who smiled and nodded, his eyes reassuring. Holly was sure he knew what the ward sister's appointment was about. She had just taken the notepad from Christine when David said in a cool voice, 'Ready, Staff?'

'When you are, sir.' Holly was icily polite.

The round had run smoothly until Holly took over. But now David drew her attention to every fault. 'Where are Mr Smith's blood results?' 'Why aren't Mr Maddison's X-rays here?'

Holly was annoyed at his scathing tone. Christine was responsible for seeing the case-notes were up to date. He was embarrassing her in front of the students, but she couldn't defend herself without revealing Christine's inefficiencies. So she just glared at him and, turning to Jean, said, 'Just pop to the office, would you, Nurse, and see if Mr Adams's biopsy report is on the desk?' the next time David complained.

Her politeness was in sharp contrast to David's brusqueness, and she noticed a faint blush tinge his cheeks. It must have made him realise how unfair he was being, for the round continued without further friction.

Christine returned as they were leaving the last bed. Holly explained the treatment changes as they stood at the office door. She carried on with the routine work then. When she came out of the side-ward she saw Christine and David talking at the end of the ward corridor, so took the opportunity to enter the office, thinking it would be empty, but Johnny Simpson was still there, writing up the notes. He looked up as she came in.

'About the dance,' he said. He threw the notes he had been writing on to the desk and stood up. 'Will you have me?' he asked, smiling at her.

She grinned. 'Yes, please.'

'I'll pick you up at your house, then, madam.'

She laughed. 'You don't need to. I'll be at Mike's flat.'

'OK.' She followed him into the corridor. 'Seven-thirty, then?' he said.

'Fine.'

The dance was on Saturday. It was Holly's duty weekend and the ward was busy; the icy weather had caused quite a few accidents. It was seven o'clock before she reached Mike's flat. He had given her a key, so she let herself in, saying, 'It's only me,' in case he should be there.

A shadowy figure appeared in the hall, too big for Mike; it was David. He didn't ask what she was doing in his brother's flat; he just said, 'I'd like to apologise properly.' He was wearing evening dress and looked magnificent—tall, distinguished and unapproachable. 'There hasn't been an opportunity on the ward, and I didn't think you would want me to call at the house, so when Mike told me you were spending the night here I thought I'd wait for you.' He took a step forward. The light shone directly over his head, haloing it. 'I'm very sorry. I shouldn't have assumed. . .' He splayed his hands. He didn't complete the sentence; it wasn't necessary.

She didn't quite know what to say. He looked so forbidding in his formal attire, and it matched his expression, so she just said, 'Thank you.'

She hated the emotional distance that lay between them. It was up to her to bridge it, and she was just about to do so when the bell rang. Turning, she opened the door. Johnny Simpson stood there.

'Not ready yet? I can see I'll have to become a fairy godmother and change Cinders into a princess.' Then he saw David. 'Oh. Er—good evening, sir.'

David acknowledged the greeting, then said to Holly, 'I'll see you at the dance.'

He passed so close to her that his jacket brushed her arm, and just this touch sent a longing through her.

Holly ignored the question in Johnny's eyes as he closed the door.

'I'll be as quick as I can,' she promised, avoiding his eyes.

Holly was in the bath when she heard Mike bang the front door, then growl outside the bathroom, 'Who's that bathing in my bath?'

She laughed. 'Ginger-locks,' she called.

'Well, hurry up or big bad Mike will come and get you.'

Holly dried herself quickly and slipped on her dressing-gown. Waves of perfumed air followed her as she left the bathroom. Mike came from the lounge, sniffing the air appreciatively.

'Hm. The old homestead has never before smelled so sweet.'

She smiled as she passed him. At the dressing-table she carefully applied her make-up. A delicate brown to her eyelids drew attention to their greenness; a touch of blusher coloured her cheeks; a delicate pink reddened her lips.

Throwing aside her dressing-gown, she slipped on her dress. She had bought it last year for the ball then, but had thought it too sophisticated and had not worn it. But now she felt it was just right. It clung to her slimmed figure, showing off her curves to advantage. The narrow straps crossed at the back. It was a shining emerald-green. She gathered her hair behind in a clip so that it cascaded down.

She looked in the mirror and was surprised. A beautiful mature woman stared back at her. She put golden earrings, which had been her mother's, into her lobes. They added just the right touch.

A bang on the bedroom door, followed by Johnny's voice calling impatiently, 'Come on, Holly,' made her slip on shoes matching the colour of her dress, snatch up a black velvet cape and clutch-bag and leave the room.

Both men turned as she entered the lounge, obvious admiration glowing on their faces. Johnny gave a wolf-whistle and Mike said in a puzzled tone, 'There's something different about you.'

Holly blushed. Johnny leapt forward to assist with her cloak. 'Are you coming with us?' he asked Mike as he settled it on her shoulders.

'No. Angie's not off until nine. We'll see you later.'

The snow that had threatened all day, and which had started when Holly had arrived at the flat, was now an inch deep.

'Oh, no,' she said, glancing at her shoes. 'I forgot to bring my boots.'

'Never mind. You wait there while I open the car door.'

He hurried over to a blue Mini, almost slipping in his haste, but righting himself with a laugh.

Suddenly Holly was glad he was taking her to the dance. His easygoing good humour was just what she needed. He unlocked the passenger-door and carefully made his way back.

'Ready?'

Before she could reply he had scooped her into his arms and was carrying her to the car. They were laughing so much that he nearly slipped again. As he took his seat beside her he wiped imaginary sweat from his brow. 'Phew,' he groaned, causing Holly to laugh again.

Why couldn't she love someone uncomplicated like Johnny, instead of David—complex, mature, magnificent?

If Johnny had not come when he had, what would have happened? Would David dance with her?

The ball was held in one of the best hotels in

Harrington. Johnny drew up at the entrance and gave an exaggerated sigh of relief when he saw that the steps leading up to the hotel were clear of snow.

'Don't think I could have repeated that carry,' he said, grinning.

Holly gave him a playful punch and laughed. His cheerfulness was infectious and she felt more lighthearted than she had for some time.

As Holly approached the hotel she loosened her cloak a little. She pushed through the swing doors, which caught the black material and pulled it from her shoulders, jerking her backwards. Only a strong hand grasping her arm prevented her falling into the door.

'Are you all right?' David set her on her feet and peered into her startled face.

She just stopped herself from saying, 'Rescuing me again', and was glad her hasty tongue was learning.

'Yes, thanks to you,' she said, smiling up at him. It was the first genuine smile she had given him since he had found Andrew at her house. It was such a relief to him that he grinned back.

Christine came forward. Her dress was a shimmering pale blue, which normally would have suited her fair complexion and blonde hair, but now the colour made her look washed out.

'That could have been nasty,' Christine said a little stiffly.

Before Holly could reply Johnny swung through the door, carrying her cape. 'Thought you'd been magicked away,' he quipped.

Holly laughed, and it was a carefree laugh, for David had smiled at her. Her whole world had changed. What had been dull and lifeless was all colour and excitement.

The four of them went into the ballroom. As Holly and Johnny joined a group of their friends, David and

Christine crossed to the tables set aside for the consultants and their guests.

Holly wondered how she could ever have thought David looked forbidding in his evening dress. He was easily the most attractive man in the room—tall, elegant, sophisticated.

'What would you like to drink?' Johnny's voice broke into her reverie.

'A Martini, please.'

Johnny was back quite quickly, considering the queue at the bar. 'One of the barmen was a patient,' he explained. 'You remember Mr Green?'

Holly thought for a moment. 'He was hit in the face with a bottle?' And, at his nod, she said, 'I couldn't forget him. He had quite a few stitches, which were difficult to take out.'

Johnny pushed her drink towards her. 'He sent you this with his compliments.'

She glanced over to the stocky man just visible behind the bar, and raised her glass. A hand saluted in reply.

Holly sipped her drink slowly, still glowing with the remembrance of David's smile. 'Come on, Holly, let's dance.' Johnny was on his feet, a hand stretched towards her.

She rose, and was about to take it when a black arm came between them. 'Consultant's privilege.' David was grinning. 'They always have the first dance.'

Johnny just smiled. David's hand was warm as it folded over hers. Her mouth was suddenly dry. She went into his arms, smiling. All her miseries slipped away and she was filled with joy. Just to be close to him was enough. She knew, he, too, was feeling the pull of their attraction. It was there in his expression, in the tightening of his arm about her, and in the desire in his eyes.

But it was more than desire with her; it was love. It burned within her, warming her whole body, flushing her face, lighting her eyes.

Did he love her? He wanted her, she knew, but did he love her? Holly looked up into his face and saw there what she wanted to see. Then doubt caught her. Maybe her need was so great that she read into his expression what she wanted to read.

He saw the uncertainty in her eyes, felt her body stiffen. 'Holly,' he whispered, his expression intense yet gentle.

Their bodies clung rather than moulded together as the soft sensuous music seemed to be playing just for them. A sense of delicious freedom released her, and she smiled lovingly up into his eyes, no longer afraid.

The tempo of the music changed. Johnny's voice broke through their cocoon. 'I know you're my boss, but you're dancing with my girl. At least, she is for this evening.'

David released Holly with a smile. 'Lucky man,' he said.

She didn't want to leave him. She wanted to stay close to him, cling to him, but she knew she couldn't. She felt as if he took part of herself with him as he went back to Christine.

Johnny swept her away. She could not concentrate on what he was saying; she was still thinking of David. Her eyes searched for him. He wasn't at the consultants' table; nor was Christine. They must be dancing. She twisted in Johnny's arms to look for them, but they weren't on the floor.

'Holly.' There was an insistence in Johnny's voice that cut through her single-minded concentration.

'Yes,' she said, looking up at him.

'You certainly seemed to be enjoying your dance with our handsome consultant.' He was eyeing her thoughtfully. 'You do know he's interested in Christine, don't you?'

'That's just hospital gossip,' she said confidently.

Holly was appalled to see pity in Johnny's eyes as he said, 'And is it hospital gossip that he spends so much time at her house?'

'How d'you know that?' She spoke more sharply than she'd intended.

'My fiancée's mother lives two houses away. I've seen his car there many a time myself.' His eyes were gentle. She had seen him look at relatives like that when he'd had bad news to impart about a patient.

Her heart beat quickly until she remembered how deceiving appearances could be. Hadn't she just experienced something similar? She took a deep breath and said, 'I seem to remember hearing that he was helping her in some way.'

'Oh?' He couldn't prevent a smile. 'Is that what they call it now?'

Holly forced a laugh. 'You shouldn't believe all you hear.'

He patted her back. 'I admire your loyalty. I just hope you're right.' He smiled kindly at her, and that made her feel worse.

The music stopped. Johnny looked over her shoulder and said, 'There's Mike and Angie.' He nodded towards the door.

They left the floor and, as they walked towards their friends, she thought, I will believe in David.

'I was late getting off,' explained Angie.

Holly hardly heard her. She was thinking of how blue David's eyes were.

'We had an emergency at quarter to nine. . .'

Holly was seeing the curve of David's lips.

'We met David on our way in,' said Mike. 'He was

taking Christine home. She seemed upset.' His eyes were compassionate.

His words acted like an alarm, sending Holly's adrenalin pumping. She could feel Johnny's eyes on her and blushed. She could guess what he was thinking—that she was the reason for the ward sister's distress.

Guilt gripped her. She wouldn't willingly upset anybody. Did Christine mean more to David than a friend?

The evening was spoilt. Destructive doubts beset her. She knew how David must have felt, and this saved her. He could not have behaved so righteously if he were Christine's lover. There must be another reason for Christine's distress. She must cling to that.

'Would you like a drink?' Angie was smiling at her.

The rest of the evening was spent by Holly wishing the ball would end. After the last dance they all went back to Mike's flat. Angie made cocoa. Holly accepted a mug and said, 'D'you mind if I go to bed? I'm on early tomorrow.'

'Today, you mean.' Mike laughed.

Holly smiled back at him, then turning to Johnny, thanked him for being her escort. She hated the compassion she saw in his eyes as he said, 'Any time. Always eager to escort a beautiful girl.'

It was some time before she fell asleep. Why had David left the dance so hurriedly with Christine? What was the reason for Christine's distress?

Doubts started to creep, insidiously, into her mind.

Eventually she slept, but her dreams were full of a white-coated figure with dark hair.

CHAPTER ELEVEN

IT WAS a heavy-eyed staff nurse who reported for duty at eight o'clock. Janet Roberts was the night staff nurse. Before Holly could even say 'Good morning,' Janet said, 'The SNO wants to see you immediately.'

Holly's eyebrows rose. She could not think of any reason for the summons. Christine had not arrived by the time the rest of the staff appeared, pale and tired but eager to tell Janet what she had missed.

'Tell Sister where I am,' said Holly. 'I'd better go.'

The SNO's office was in the administrative part of the hospital. Holly knocked, and entered on being instructed to do so.

The SNO was a grey-haired lady with a pleasant round face, which could become stern and forbidding if her nursing ideals were not upheld. All the staff under her command knew as soon as they entered the office whether they were going to be complimented or told off; Mrs Phillips's face was very expressive.

Today Holly was not sure. The lines on the SNO's features were severely set, but the eyes were kind.

'Ah, Nurse Grant.' She paused to allow Holly to approach the desk. It was placed between two tall windows, which threw light on to the person standing before it. All the nurses knew it had been placed there for that reason.

'I would like you to take charge of ward ten for the time being, as Sister Nicol will be off for a while.' Mrs Phillips's face was expressionless.

Thoughts chased each other through Holly's mind.

Was she the reason for Christine's absence? Had seeing Holly dancing with David so intimately made her ill?

'I'm sure you'll do your best, and there's always the sister on Women's Surgical to consult if you are worried.' She smiled kindly. 'I'll try and find you a staff nurse but we're short-handed at the moment because of flu, as I'm sure you know.'

'I'll manage,' Holly assured her.

Mrs Phillips's features relaxed. 'I'm sure you will.'

On the way back to the ward Holly was thinking how at one time she would have been elated to be acting sister, but now all she felt was guilt. Mixed with that feeling was the thought that she did not care how many people might criticise her conduct—that dance had been worth it. She could feel his arms about her now, as she hurried back to the ward. She would believe in him. She had to. Her happiness depended on it.

Even as these thoughts flashed through her mind, she remembered how Christine had looked at David. Little things came back to her. Catching Christine smoothing her hand over David's white coat, and blushing when she saw Holly watching her. How Christine's face would light with pleasure when David walked into the office. How the cool features would flush if he appeared unexpectedly, and the relief in Christine's voice when Andrew had arrived to take her home from Casualty. Holly had experienced such moments herself and realised that Christine was in love with David. She had been so wrapped up in her own emotional involvement that she had not admitted Christine's until now.

So we're both in love with him, Holly thought. Perhaps that was why Christine had been so hostile towards her when she had first arrived on the ward, and not because of the previous staff nurse's inefficiency. How complicated life could be.

'Sister's not here,' said Janet as Holly entered the office.

'I know.' She told them about her temporary promotion.

'We'll have to watch our step now,' teased Janet. 'You know the old saying "New brooms sweep clean".'

The young nurses tittered.

'OK, OK.' Holly took their banter with a smile. At least she had good nurses to work with. 'It looks as if we are going to be busy with one short, so we'd better get cracking.'

After the report had been taken and Janet had gone, Holly straightened her cap and said, 'It's Mr Quinn's ward round today. We don't want him thinking that we can't cope because Sister isn't here, do we?' She used the collective 'we' deliberately to pull them into a team.

'No, Staff,' the girls agreed.

Holly drew the treatment book towards her, noting that Christine had added a bowel wash-out for Mr Wick. She delegated the nurses their duties and, after they had left, breathed a sigh of relief.

Holly was surprised at how tense she was. She had been in charge of the ward many times before, so there should not be a difference now, but there was. On those other occasions Christine had always been there to consult by phone if Holly became worried, not that she had ever needed to avail herself of the ward sister's kindness. Would she be capable enough? Had she the experience? There was always the sister on Women's Surgical to refer to.

Taking comfort from this thought, she rose from the chair. The postie's black head came round the door after a perfunctory knock.

'Hi, "Sister",' he said, grinning, his hands full of letters.

'News certainly travels fast.' She took them from him with a smile.

He laughed and closed the door behind him.

Holly went over to the case-note trolley to re-check that they were all in order. She did not want David. . . A vision of him, striding through this very door, immaculate in spotless white coat, his university tie lying flat against a white shirt, rose in her mind. Would he smile? Would his eyes hold a message for her? Or had he been at Christine's?

Holly pushed these thoughts aside but her hand trembled as she took out the first folder.

By ten o'clock the ward was ready. As she went from patient to patient, checking the chart at the foot of their bed and casting an eye over the lockers, she suddenly cheered up. This was what she wanted to do. She must stop thinking about David and concentrate on her job.

Holly had reached the ward door when she glimpsed a flash of white through the glass porthole. In spite of her resolve, she could not help but feel a tremor of anticipation. Her eye brightened, her step quickened.

The back of a white coat greeted her as she entered the office. The black-haired figure swung round. It was with sharp disappointment that she saw Richard Morris, the registrar. His build and colouring were roughly the same as David's.

'I hear you've a temporary promotion. Congratulations.' He had a cool, contained face which gave little away. He was a competent but not dedicated doctor.

Holly acknowledged his felicitation, not sure whether he was being sarcastic or not.

'David won't be here today, so we can start the round.'

Holly was pulling the trolley forward when the door swung wide, nearly hitting her.

'Sorry!' exclaimed Johnny. 'I didn't hurt you, did I?'

'No. It was probably my fault. I had the trolley too near the door.'

'If you two have stopped apologising,' the registrar's dry voice drawled, 'we can get on with the round.'

There was a noticeable difference in the patients' response to Richard Morris. They were subdued. There were no little jokes from him, no sitting on the bed to listen with kind eyes to their worries the way David did.

One of the men, a Mr Thomas who had had his inguinal hernia repaired, was told he would be fit for work a month following his discharge the next day.

'I've been made redundant,' he told the registrar.

'So have many others,' Richard replied airily, and moved to the next bed.

David would have known that Mr Thomas was out of work. He would have sat down and talked to the patient, discussed his problems, offered suggestions for re-employment. David treated the whole person, not just the ailment.

Holly's expression must have shown what she was thinking, for the registrar said arrogantly, 'The social services deal with these problems.'

She just prevented herself from giving a scathing reply. Turning away, she picked out the next patient's notes.

The round was finished more quickly than usual.

'Very efficient, Staff,' Richard complimented her when they entered the office. 'An improvement on the rounds of late.'

Holly resented his reference to Christine's lapses. They were alone in the office. Johnny had stayed in the ward, Holly suspected, to speak with Mr Thomas.

'Sister Nicol is an excellent ward sister,' she said, her eyes angry.

Richard Morris's face tightened. 'Quite the little spitfire, aren't we?' he sneered. 'No wonder our consultant was drooling over you at the dance.' He raised an eyebrow. 'All that pent-up passion.' There was no mistaking his implication, or the salacious expression in his eyes.

Holly was so shocked by his remark that she was speechless for a moment. Then she said, looking him straight in the eye, 'I find your remark extremely offensive.' The contempt in her voice was obvious, and she had the pleasure of seeing a faint blush stain Richard Morris's cheeks.

He opened his mouth to reply, but Johnny came into the office. He glanced from one to the other but did not say anything, assuming that Holly's hasty tongue had made trouble for her again. He had drawn out the chair and was about to sit in it to write up the notes when Richard said roughly, his voice cold, 'You can do those after we have done the round on the female ward.'

'See you later,' whispered Johnny as he passed Holly.

She was so upset by the registrar's comments that she could not even smile in reply. Sitting down at the desk after they had gone, she sighed. If Richard Morris thought like that, gossip would be rife. Well, there was nothing she could do about that, so she'd better get on with her work.

The sister from Women's Surgical came over later that morning to check the dangerous drugs with Holly. Normally a pleasant, friendly woman, today her face was serious, and Holly wondered if it was disapproval of her that had caused the sister to be so solemn. I'm being paranoid, she thought, and hurried away to do a linen-count.

It was a busy day for Holly. Not only did she have

the routine work to do, but she wanted to check on the ward stock as well.

She had lunch in the canteen. A few interested glances were cast her way as she ate on her own.

By four-thirty, Holly felt she had brought the ward back to its previous standard. Lotions, dressing packs, bandages and micropore had all been ordered; the emergency trolley had been stripped and washed down; suction machine tested, catheters and intravenous sets inspected; all the emergency drugs checked that they were in date.

At six o'clock she was ready to go off, feeling satisfied with her efforts. She hurried to Mike's flat, packed her things quickly and, leaving the key on the mantelpiece, closed the door behind her.

A bus came just as she reached the stop. Secure in her own home, sitting by the fire, curtains drawn against the cold night, she relaxed and was comforted. Her father's presence seemed very strong in the house that night. It was as if he was telling her not to worry.

The following day she was glad of the responsibility; it prevented her from thinking. The SNO had not managed to send a staff nurse to help, but had sent a junior nurse who needed to be initiated into the ward routine, taking up more of Holly's time.

Half an hour for lunch was all she allowed herself. She was spooning her soup when Angie put her tray down opposite and sat down.

'I was terribly sorry to hear the news,' she said, setting her dishes out on the table.

Some of the soup slopped off Holly's spoon. Apprehension filled her eyes. 'What news?' she asked as she mopped up the splash with her serviette.

'Haven't you heard?' Angie's voice was astonished.

'No,' said Holly sharply.

'Christine Nicol's brother died last night.' Angie's

eyes were sombre. 'Apparently she received a phone call at the dance to say his condition had deteriorated. Nobody knew he was ill. Even Mike didn't know.' She sounded aggrieved. 'He had AIDS and was being nursed at home.'

Holly's immediate thought was relief that she was not the reason for Christine's distress. Thoughts whirled in her head. That must have been the reason for Christine's lack of concentration and for her tiredness. Her eyes became sad. She knew how Christine must be feeling. Her own grief was still fresh.

Angie left her soup untasted. 'I'm surprised you didn't know. She is your ward sister.'

'But we weren't close.' Holly sounded defensive. 'I would have thought David would have told Mike.'

'Yes, you would,' agreed Angie. 'Especially as Christine's brother was David's friend.'

So that was the friend David had spoken about.

'I think Christine didn't want anybody to know, not because she was ashamed but because she's a very private person,' Holly defended her ward sister. She rose. 'I must go.'

Angie looked at the unfinished soup in her friend's bowl. 'But you've hardly eaten anything.'

'We're short-staffed.' Holly made this her excuse. She did not say that her appetite had left her.

Back in the office, Holly wondered about David. Had he told her the truth when he had said Christine was just a friend? Johnny's pitying face rose to torment her, and there was that hairpin she had found in David's flat.

A vision of him taking that pin from Christine's blonde hair made her hastily leave the office and search out the third-year nurse to tell her to go for lunch. Anything to distract her thoughts.

Holly was writing in the Kardex when the phone

rang. It was Casualty. 'The registrar's just seen a patient with a very nasty neck abcess. He thinks it should be opened under a general anaesthetic tonight, so we're sending him up to you. His name's Matthew Harrison.'

'Thanks, Staff.'

Holly had just made out a temperature and Kardex card when a nurse appeared at the office door with the patient.

'Mr Harrison,' she said, handing Holly the notes.

A middle-aged man with an angry face said, 'I'm sure I could have gone home and come back tomorrow.' His voice was cross.

Holly observed the flushed face, the over-bright eyes and the severely inflamed swelling on his neck, and said firmly, 'I'm sure you could have, Mr Harrison, but I think your headache would have become worse.' She smiled kindly.

His anger changed to astonishment. 'How did you know I had a headache?'

'With a swelling like that. . .' She left the sentence unfinished.

Mr Harrison smiled ruefully.

'I think you'll feel a lot better when this. . .' she gestured towards his lump '. . .is opened.'

Beckoning to Jean Bailey, she said, 'Put Mr Harrison in bed two, will you, Nurse, please? And place a "nil by mouth" notice over it.'

'What about my wife?' The patient was looking anxious.

Holly gave him a reassuring smile. 'I'll phone her and let her know you've been admitted.'

Holly could hear him grumbling to Jean as they went into the ward. 'I only came for a plaster.'

Holly phoned Mrs Harrison and explained gently the reason for her husband's admission.

'I'll bring in his pyjamas and shaving gear,' was the calm reply. 'I told him to see the doctor, but you know what men are.'

Holly laughed. She had just put down the receiver when a shadow fell across the desk. 'I believe you've admitted a new patient.' It was David.

Holly looked up at him. His face was drawn and tired, his eyes sombre. She rose, longing to touch him, smooth away his sadness as he had hers, but he seemed distant.

She handed him Mr Harrison's notes. 'Mr Morris plans to incise the abcess at about ten o'clock. Triplopen was given in Casualty.'

David opened the folder; there was only one sheet.

'Good.' He snapped it shut and handed it back to her. 'Does the theatre know?'

'Yes.'

Why had he come? she wondered. It was just a small operation. Johnny could have done it. Then she knew. David needed her as she had needed him.

'I'm so sorry about your friend, David.' She was unable to stop the tears brightening her eyes.

He sank into the chair beside the desk and rested his head on his hand and closed his eyes. Holly noticed that his shirt was creased, his tie slack. He probably had not been to bed. She had felt compassion before but never so deeply.

Putting an arm about his shoulders, she held him close. He looked up at her. 'If you could have seen him, Holly.' The rims of his eyes were red. 'Wasted like an old man, and he was only thirty-two.' Disbelief sharpened his voice. 'He had his whole life before him.'

Her arms tightened about him. 'Oh, Holly. It was so dreadful, so pathetic.' She could feel him tremble, and stroked his hair, her face wet with the tears he could not shed.

She didn't say the usual things—'Time will heal', 'It was a happy release'. She knew from her own experience that grief was something no one could help with.

Eventually his trembling stopped. 'Christine is very upset. She had hoped Hammond Hall would be ready to take him.' He glanced up at her. 'That's what we were doing that day you had trouble with your eye—looking for a suitable property.'

Holly remembered, and also recalled how she had assumed the couple had been looking for a home for themselves.

'It will benefit others,' she said gently. 'And perhaps, in time, that will comfort her.'

'Yes.' The dullness in his eyes lightened. He reached for her hands. 'You're very wise, Holly.' His voice was soft and deep.

Holly found his intense gaze disconcerting and said, to break the tension, 'Would you like a cup of tea?' removing her hands from his.

David took a deep breath and rose to his feet. 'No, thanks. I must go.' He was so close that she could see the weave of his tie. Putting his hands on her shoulders, he said, 'Thanks for comforting me.'

She smiled. 'That's what nurses are for,' she quipped, hoping to take the sadness from his face by being facetious.

But instead of smiling his expression remained sombre. 'Is that what you want, Holly? To be a career woman? Do you intend to be a Florence Nightingale all your life? What about love, husband, children?' His eyes were wistful.

Holly was stunned for a moment. Then she understood. He must have supposed that that was why she had not responded to his offer of love that day they were painting. Why he had felt rejected.

She raised her hands and smoothed the lapels of his

jacket, not looking at him. 'Can't I have both?' she whispered. Then looked up at him and smiled.

His expression changed dramatically. Delight swept the sad lines from his face. He lost ten years in a moment.

'If that's a proposal, I accept.' He grinned cheekily and wrapped his arms round her.

It had happened so quickly that she was breathless.

'David,' she whispered, and the way that she spoke his name told him all he wanted to know.

His lips came down upon hers in a kiss that sealed their commitment. It was not passionate, yet it promised passion. They were on duty. Loving would have to wait. He took her face in his hands and said, 'We've a lot to talk about. When are you off?'

'At six, if we're not busy,' she said, her eyes shining with happiness.

'I'll meet you in the car park. We can go to your house or my flat for our. . .' he smiled outrageously '. . .talk.'

She blushed and laughed. 'I think Sheeplaw is a good idea.' She didn't want to start their relationship in the severe surroundings of his flat. She wanted the happy ambience of her home to bless them.

'So do I.' He said it so quietly, with such a loving expression in his eyes, that she flung her arms round his neck and kissed him.

'I do like that,' he said, grinning, his arms tightening about her.

But, even though she knew how delighted he was, she sensed a lingering sadness behind his carefree words and reached up her face to kiss him, wishing she could take away his grief.

He released her reluctantly. 'I'll see you in the car park at six, then,' he said, and kissed the tip of her nose.

After he had gone the office still seemed to be filled with his presence. She hugged the knowledge that he loved her to herself, even though no word had been spoken.

Jean came into the office, saying, 'Mr Harrison has settled down. Found the man in the next bed was a neighbour.'

It took Holly a moment to bring herself down from her cloud. 'Good,' she said, sure that Jean would notice the glowing happiness on her face and say something, but the junior nurse just took the temperature chart and left.

Holly had to concentrate very hard on her work during the rest of her time on duty. She thought she had succeeded until one of the patients said, 'You must be in love, Staff. You've already taken my temperature.'

Holly smiled and blushed, but made no comment.

Nothing prevented her from going off at six. There were patches of ice outside the hospital, so she had to walk carefully. Snow was forecast. The lights in the car park seemed brighter because of the frost. Tiny twinkles looked up at her from the patches.

David left the car and opened the passenger-door for her. The inside light flicked on and off like a camera flash.

They spoke little as they drove. Flakes of snow started as they left Harrington behind them.

'We should have gone to your flat,' she said anxiously. 'I had forgotten about the weather forecast.'

'It probably won't fall for very long,' he reassured her.

But what had started as a light flurry became heavy before they reached Sheeplaw, and David had to drive very slowly.

There was a garage beside the house but it still held

her father's car. David drove his into the small drive in front of the garage door.

Holly left him to lock the car while she opened the front door. Even that short distance covered them with snow. They were laughing as they brushed it off each other in the hall. They hung their coats side by side on the hall stand beside one of her father's that she had left to comfort her.

Shivering, more from anticipation than the cold, she opened the lounge door. Mrs Braithwaite had drawn the curtains. Holly lit the gas fire; its glow added to the cosiness of the room.

'You've made a good job of this,' said David, gesturing round the room.

Cretonnes in pink and green, covering the three-piece suite, drew out the green in the carpet and curtains. The wooden mantelpiece was polished and shining. The pink lampshades were the same colour as the walls.

'You've repainted the walls,' he said, admiring the muted shade.

'Yes. The white was too cold for winter.

Tension underlay the banality of their remarks. It was as if they were deliberately delaying their coming together, as if they had been journeying towards a place of lightness and exaltation which, if held back, would be all the sweeter.

They were standing facing one another, not touching. The expression in his eyes filled her with so great an emotion that she was unable to speak. He read what she would have said in her expression. David held out his hand and she placed hers in it. The smile on their faces was a recognition that they knew they were loved, and by each other.

She went into his arms lovingly.

'Holly, Holly,' he whispered, holding her close. 'I love you.'

Never had three words sounded so sweet. 'And I love you.' Tears sprang to her eyes.

He kissed them away, and when his lips touched hers it was gently, tentatively. He didn't want to frighten her; he loved her too much. He drew her down on to the couch and held her in his arms.

'I thought perhaps. . . Christine. . .?' She started to put into words her doubts.

'No.' He shook his head. 'It was never Christine, it was always you, but I thought you didn't want me; I thought you wanted a younger man, or that you wanted a career.' His eyes were vulnerable.

She smiled and kissed him. 'No. It was always you,' she said, and laughed as she repeated his words. 'That time in this room. . .' she glanced at the walls '. . . I was so frightened of losing you as I had lost my father that I let that precious moment slip and it gave you the wrong impression.' She shivered at the remembered distress. His arms tightened. 'And then that fiasco with Andrew finished everything.' She could laugh at it now, secure in his embrace.

He kissed her, and this time there was passion in his lips. She responded eagerly, unashamedly. She wanted him to know that her desire was as strong as his.

Breathlessly they drew apart. 'This is going to be a short engagement,' he said, laughter in his voice. 'I want all of you and all the time.'

'Really, Doctor.' She blushed and laughed. Then her face became serious. 'I think Christine's in love with you,' she blurted out.

He sighed. 'Perhaps, but she knows I'm in love with you. She's leaving.' A sadness crept into his voice. 'She's going to take charge of Hammond Hall.' He kissed away the worry-lines on her face and smiled gently down at her. 'I think I should see what the weather's doing.'

Arms about each other, they went to the front door. It was snowing hard. They looked at each other and laughed. It was as if the weather had conspired to maroon them, as if the moors were working magic on their behalf.

They spent the evening smiling a lot, laughing a lot, eating a little. Then they went to bed, their plans for the future made. And in the softness of the double bed they committed themselves to each other with a passion that almost consumed them.

When they lay at peace in each other's arms, Holly knew her life had changed completely. A light had come into her life which would burn brightly and which only death could extinguish. At that thought a shadow crossed her face, and she shivered.

'Don't be frightened, my love. Death will never part us.' He had guessed the reason for her distress. 'I think it's time I kissed you again.' There was a mischievous twinkle in his eyes. 'Just to comfort you, of course.'

She laughed and her fears disappeared. And as their kiss deepened she knew he was right. Their love would last beyond life.

Mills & Boon
BRING YOU COMFORT & JOY FOR CHRISTMAS

Four heart-warming Medical Romances in a single volume.

CHRISTMAS PRESENT
Lynne Collins

THE WAY WE WERE
Laura MacDonald

A MIRACLE OR TWO
Marion Lennox

THE REAL CHRISTMAS MESSAGE
Sharon Wirdnam

Available from November 1991, priced at £3.99

Available from Boots, Martins, John Menzies, W. H. Smith, and other paperback stockists.
Also available from Mills & Boon Reader Service, P.O. Box 236, Thornton Road, Croydon, Surrey, CR9 3RU.

A special gift for Christmas

Four romantic stories by four of your favourite authors for you to unwrap and enjoy this Christmas.

Robyn Donald — STORM OVER PARADISE
Catherine George — BRAZILIAN ENCHANTMENT
Emma Goldrick — SMUGGLER'S LOVE
Penny Jordan — SECOND-BEST HUSBAND

Published on 11th October, 1991   Price: £6.40

Mills & Boon

Available from Boots, Martins, John Menzies, W.H. Smith, and other paperback stockists.

Also available from Mills and Boon Reader Service, P.O. Box 236, Thornton Road, Croydon, Surrey CR9 3RU.

4 MEDICAL ROMANCES AND 2 FREE GIFTS
From Mills & Boon

Capture all the excitement, intrigue and emotion of the busy medical world by accepting four FREE Medical Romances, plus a FREE cuddly teddy and special mystery gift. Then if you choose, go on to enjoy 4 more exciting Medical Romances every month! Send the coupon below at once to:

> MILLS & BOON READER SERVICE, FREEPOST
> PO BOX 236, CROYDON, SURREY CR9 9EL.
> No stamp required

-- ✂ -- -- -- -- -- -- -- -- -- -- -- -- -- -- -- ✂ --

YES! Please rush me my 4 Free Medical Romances and 2 Free Gifts! Please also reserve me a Reader Service Subscription. If I decide to subscribe, I can look forward to receiving 4 Medical Romances every month for just £5.80 delivered direct to my door. Post and packing is free, and there's a free Mills & Boon Newsletter. If I choose not to subscribe I shall write to you within 10 days – I can keep the books and gifts whatever I decide. I can cancel or suspend my subscription at any time. I am over 18.

EP02D

Name (Mr/Mrs/Ms) _____

Address _____

_____

_____ Postcode _____

Signature _____

Offer expires **31st December 1991**. The right is reserved to refuse an application and change the terms of this offer. Readers overseas and in Eire please send for details. Southern Africa write to Independent Book Services, Postbag X3010, Randburg 2125. You may be mailed with offers from other reputable companies as a result of this application. If you would prefer not to share in this opportunity, please tick box. ☐

Mills & Boon

— MEDICAL ROMANCE —

The books for your enjoyment this month are:

A SPECIAL CHALLENGE Judith Ansell
HEART IN CRISIS Lynne Collins
DOCTOR TO THE RESCUE Patricia Robertson
BASE PRINCIPLES Sheila Danton

♥ ♥ ♥ ♥ ♥

Treats in store!

Watch next month for the following absorbing stories:

MEDICAL DECISIONS Lisa Cooper
DEADLINE LOVE Judith Worthy
NO TIME FOR ROMANCE Kathleen Farrell
RELATIVE ETHICS Caroline Anderson

Available from Boots, Martins, John Menzies, W.H. Smith and other paperback stockists.

Also available from Reader Service, P.O. Box 236, Thornton Road, Croydon, Surrey CR9 3RU.

Readers in South Africa — write to:
Independent Book Services Pty, Postbag X3010, Randburg, 2125, S. Africa.